RETURN TO
THE
SAME CITY

*Novels of Paco Ignacio Taibo II
in English translation:*

RETURN TO
THE
SAME CITY

PACO IGNACIO TAIBO II

THE MYSTERIOUS PRESS

Published by Warner Books

A Time Warner Company

Originally published in Mexico by Editoria Planeta de México

 Mysterious Press books are published by Warner Books, Inc.,
1271 Avenue of the Americas, New York, NY 10020.

 A Time Warner Company

The Mysterious Press name and logo are registered trademarks of
Warner Books, Inc.

Printed in the United States of America
First U.S. printing: September 1996
10 9 8 7 6 5 4 3 2 1

Library of Congress Cataloging-in-Publication Data

Taibo, Paco Ignacio
    [Regreso a la misma ciudad y bajo la lluvia. English]
    Return to the same city / Paco Ignacio Taibo II.
        p.   cm.
    ISBN 0-89296-590-8
    I. Title.
PQ7298.3.A58R413   1996
863—dc20   96-14425
                                                       CIP

For my colleague Roger Simon aka Rogelio Simón, who inducted the Lakers into the known religions and placed Moses Wine on my path.

For my colleague Andreu Martín, who clearly delights in writing novels as much as I do.

For my colleague Pérez Valero, who clearly suffers as much as I do.

For colleague Dick Lochte, who lent his name to a character.

For colleagues Ross Thomas and Joe Gores, who will appear as the owners of a brothel in Tijuana in my next novel.

To these, my friends, a novel for the ones they have given me, with the reader's gratitude.

A Note from the Author

Don't ask me when and how Héctor Belascoarán Shayne came back to life. I don't have an answer. I remember that on the last page of *No Happy Ending* rain was falling over his perforated body. His appearance in these pages is therefore an act of magic. White magic perhaps, but magic that is irrational and disrespectful toward the occupation of writing a mystery series.

The magic is not entirely my fault. Appeal to the cultural traditions of a country whose history teems with resurrections. Here Dracula returned, El Santo returned (in the film version), even Demetrio Vallejo returned from prison, Benito Juárez returned from Paso del Norte... This particular resurrection gestated a couple of years ago in the city of Zacatecas, when the audience of a conference demanded that Belascoarán come back to life almost (minus one vote) unanimously. From then on, that event would repeat itself several more times before various audiences in different cities, and the voting was accompanied by a long series of letters. It seemed that the character had not found an ending to the liking of his readers, and the author thought there were a few stories left to be told in the Belascoaránian saga. And thus was born this novel, which if it has any virtue, it is because it was written with even more doubts than the previous ones. So let the readers from Zacatecas who attended that conference be as responsible as I am for Héctor's return.

I have no better explanation.

As always, it must be said that the story told here belongs to the terrain of absolute fiction, although Mexico is the same and belongs to the terrain of surprising reality.

It would have to be added that for narrative reasons, real times have been slightly rearranged, uniting the student protests of early '87 with the ascent of the Cuauhtémoc Cárdenas campaign of the spring of '88, in a fictional time that could be situated around the end of 1987.

PIT II
Mexico City, 1987–88–89

Each resurrection will make you lonelier.

—César Dávila Andrade

RETURN TO THE SAME CITY

I

The only rush is that of the heart.

Silvio Rodríguez

"How many times have you died?"

"Uhm," said the woman with the ponytail, and indicated *none* with her head.

"Me, yes. A lot."

She passed her index finger over the scars that made little patterns on his chest. Héctor gently withdrew her hand and, naked, walked toward the window. It was a cold night. The filtered Delicados were on the window-sill; he drew the flame of the lighter into the tip of one, and watched the green lights that the streetlights threw on the trees.

"No, not the scars; that's not what I'm saying. I'm saying sleep, going to sleep and dying again. A hundred, two hundred times in a year. The first fucking instant of sleep is not sleep, it's dying again."

"You only die once."

"James Bond must have said that. You die a ton of times. Son of a bitch. I know what it is ... Sometimes I wish I could sleep with my eyes open so as not to die. If you sleep with your eyes open, you can never die."

"Dead people end up with their eyes open," she said after a pause, turning away. Her bottom shone like the foliage of the trees out front.

"Those dead people die just once. No. I'm talking about dying a lot. Two or three times a week at least."

"What is your death like?"

Héctor stood there thinking. When he spoke again, the woman with the ponytail could not see his face, but she could hear the abnormally hoarse voice with which he told his story.

"You can't breathe. You feel fire in your stomach. You can't move the fingers on your hand. You've got your face stuck in a puddle and your lips fill up with dirty water. You shit in your pants, you can't help it. The blood coming out your nose is mixing with the water of the puddle . . . It's raining."

"Now?"

"No, when you die."

She remained silent for a moment, wanting to look somewhere else. The light in the window illuminated the scars on Héctor's chest.

"Dead people don't tell these stories."

"That's what you think," Héctor said, without looking at her.

"Dead people don't make love."

"A whole bunch of live people I know don't either. They're screwed that way, they've been put on a diet."

Héctor moved away from the window and crossed in front of the bed. She turned again to look at him, the ponytail falling between her breasts.

"Do you want a drink?" Héctor asked, walking down

the hall toward the kitchen. The cold rose up inside him through the soles of his feet.

"Could you make decaffeinated?"

"You ask a lot."

"For a guy who's died so often, making decaf should be a cinch."

"Definitely not, a decaf is a decaf and a cinch a cinch. The decaf is much more complicated."

Héctor came back with a Coke in one hand, a lime split down the middle balancing between the fingers of the other. He sought out the window again.

"It's raining," he said as he squeezed the lime and gently stirred the rind so it would mix in.

"When you die?"

"No, now," he said, and he stepped aside to avoid being hit in the head with a copy of Malraux's *Man's Fate* which she had thrown at him.

Héctor smiled.

"Cover your nakedness, woman, here comes the icy wind."

He opened the window. Indeed, a cold wind forced the rain into the room. One big drop hit him on the nose and trickled over his mustache. He opened his mouth and swallowed it.

"There it is," said the woman with the ponytail, smiling. "Dead people can't taste rain."

"You might be right. It's just a matter of keeping the eyes open and of convincing the Japanese man I've got in here," he pointed to his temple with his index finger, making the universal sign for suicide.

"You've got Quasimodo in your head. And he spends his time ringing the bells of Notre-Dame."

"And screwing the Japanese man with whom he shares the apartment. In fact, the Japanese guy must be the one who controls the sound and protects the transistors."

"I never should have fallen in love with a Mexican detective."

"You never should have fallen in love with a dead man."

Suddenly, with no forewarning, she started to cry; wrapped up to her chin, covering herself from the cold and from the one-eyed, skinny, mustached detective before her, who made a face intended to be a loving smile, but which instead was the grimace of a man who was cold and couldn't cry.

He had been going back to the office for only a week, refamiliarizing himself with the old furniture and the old colleagues, convinced that the old habits had ended. If he didn't take down the sign on the door that read "Belascoarán Shayne, Detective," it was because El Gallo and Carlos Vargas, his officemates, threatened to open an independent detective agency the instant he retired. That stopped him. If he didn't want to be responsible for himself, he definitely didn't want to be responsible for others. He'd been walking through that entrance for seven days, sitting at his old desk, shaking off the dust a little, reading papers from two years before and lighting a candle in prayer to Sigmund Freud's mom to let no one open the door and offer him a job. A week saturated with paranoia and distrust. Irrational anxiety that came like a tropical storm and filled his palms with sweat, numbed his spine, pricked his temples. Tremendous fears, like fifty-story elevator shafts with no bottom except dementia. New fears: going to the bathroom, crossing the long hall outside the office, turning his back to the door, turning on a light in the window and leaving his silhouette outlined against the shadows on the street, answering the phone and having a strange voice speak to him familiarly.

That's why, after a week of terror that took him back to other people's childhood stories (his own had been peaceful and calm, as if between the feathers of a sparrow's nest), when the phone rang he looked to his officemates, even though he knew they weren't around. He stared at the calendars of cabaret singers' asses and blondes in beer ads, but the women in print on the wall refused to lend him a hand in answering the phone. They didn't want to take the inverse route to glory and come back from the image of the calendar to the office from which they had fled.

"Hello?"

"Señor Belascoarán, please."

"He's not here," Héctor said. "He doesn't come in anymore."

"Gracias," said the voice with a strange accent dragging that final *s.* The voice of a woman. Of a waitress from a fancy restaurant who pronounces the menu correctly. Mexican, maybe? Bolivian? Peruvian?

"You're welcome," Héctor added and hung up softly.

A quarter of an hour later, the phone rang again.

Héctor smiled.

"Hello?"

"I'd like to speak with you. You're the gentleman who answered before, right?"

"The gentleman who answered before isn't here," Héctor said. "He just left. He's retiring from this. He went to get something to drink."

"And now what does he do?" the woman asked with a little laugh.

"Buddhism. Zen contemplation. Empirical analysis of environmental pollution issues."

"Thank you," said the voice.

"You're welcome," said Héctor.

He hung up again and walked over to the safe where he stored the drinks and the firearms. *Fire*arms—not even close. A jackknife, two stale Pepsis, a collection of porn photos—graphic reminders of an old case that Gilberto, the plumber, kept like heirlooms. He grabbed the knife and put it in his pocket.

If he had had to go through a metal detector, the machine would have gone crazy with glee; not just because of the knife, but also from the echoes of a stud lodged in his femur that now could never come out, a .45 automatic in a holster around his back and a .38 short-barreled revolver in his pants pocket. "Iron man," he said to himself. A metallurgical piece of work is what he was.

The phone rang again.

"Could we meet?" asked the woman with the Peruvian? Bolivian? Chilean? Mexican? accent.

"Do we know each other?"

"I do, yes, I know you a little."

"What kind of bra do you wear?"

"Why?"

"No, nothing. It was to see if we knew each other," Héctor said, playing with the knife. "I now see that we don't."

He hung up again and left the office, putting on his black sheepskin jacket. The phone was ringing as he walked out the door.

Now more than ever he had the absurd ability to feel out of place everywhere. It was something new: to be an eternal observer, to be invariably on the outside. When you don't own them, landscapes can be observed with much greater precision, but you're also alien to the panorama, unable to touch the ground, to feel the breeze. The sensation of strangeness is permanent. A shadow running through other people's lands, an actor in a borrowed scene and in the wrong play, a Western movie character in an Italian comedy. The emptiness could come at any moment, intensifying the normal sensation of being out of place. It could happen to him in the lobby of the Bellas Artes Palace during the intermission of the opera, as easily as at a dinner of the '65–'67 high school class, as in the mattress display room in the Vázquez brothers' furniture stores, as in the line to buy tortillas. The things were there, he was there, but they didn't belong to him. At some point someone would arrive and ask to see his ticket, his visiting permit, his passport, the credentials that gave him the right to a discount that he didn't have. This sensation of slipping through life was particularly agonizing in elevators and in supermarkets. Héctor couldn't explain why, but that's the way it was. He felt that one moment or another, the apparatus would stop on the third floor and he would be amiably asked to get off; or the supermarket's cops would stop him from passing through the checkout with his cart, because the bills with which he wanted to pay were no longer legal currency.

Yet the obsession didn't seem to produce external symptoms. It didn't contort his face or make his eye red. The messenger, with his yellow helmet and pile of envelopes, and the cleaning lady with the bucket of water didn't pay him the slightest attention. They didn't even give him a second glance. Maybe they were experiencing the same thing he was, and that's why he didn't seem strange to them; we were all a bunch of unconfessed lepers, all Victoria Holt trying unsuccessfully to imitate F. Scott Fitzgerald.

He got off on the sixth floor and dodged the front desk, going directly to the cashier's window. The cashier had caught her stocking on a desk drawer and took a while to notice him. Héctor lit a cigarette and watched her manipulate stockings and drawer.

"*Ay,*" she said, finally making eye contact with the ex-detective. "Your check?"

Héctor nodded, leaving the remains of a smile floating. The girl finally managed to disentangle herself, looked for the check in an enormous folder and walked backward toward the window, trying to hide her ruined stocking, with a consequently quite hunchbacked stride. Héctor signed the papers, took the check, and left without looking at her again.

He walked between the little shops on Insurgentes, crossed the subway stop at a sluggish pace, turned at Chapultepec Avenue, absorbing the city's billboards with his healthy eye. Human misery was striking in the pandemonium of the pre-Christmas season. Under-employment was running rampant. A wave of Mexicans, with sad and feverish eyes, in search of a peso attacked from all sides. The begging hands of charity were more chapped, more tremulous than usual. How to be at one with all this? Héctor asked himself. How to coexist with this without rotting in sadness? he wondered again. Elisa had once read aloud something Cortázar wrote about the train station in New Delhi and the sensation he'd been filled with—that you cannot co-habitate with certain dark regions of this world without becoming a little cynical, turning into a real son of a bitch—came back to him. Cortázar was right. In the language of the 1950s, there was no peaceful coexis-tence with the part of society that was falling apart, with that other part of you that was sinking. For a one-eyed man it should be easier, you only have to close one eye, he said to himself, and he didn't dare even smile at the joke.

He walked down Chapultepec in search of calm and found it in a butcher shop and in a travel agency, his two points of intimate contact with consumer society. By the time he got to his brother's house, an apartment building with a rusty facade on Sinaloa Street, he wanted a loin sausage and a fourteen-day trip to Manila.

The door to Apartment C was open. That was unusual and Héctor reacted immediately, putting his hand on the holster of the gun over his heart. Carlos's voice from the kitchen reassured him.

"Come in, stupid. The door's open because Marina went to the store to buy drinks."

Carlos was correcting galleys at the kitchen table, disheveled and in a T-shirt. A Vivaldi concerto was ending on the record player. After the crackling of the needle, a Russian chorus started to sing the Internationale.

"That's the sign that it's time for vermouth," Carlos said, and he got up, brushing the bread crumbs off his jeans. "How is your reencounter with life treating you?"

"Okay," Héctor said, disinclined to provide explanations.

"Take it slowly."

"I'm trying."

Carlos served himself a vermouth on the rocks, taking the bottle and the ice from the refrigerator. It didn't even occur to him to offer one to his brother.

"You don't look very good. You make me want to put a glass of milk down in front of you."

Héctor made his best bewildered face. No worries. No melodrama. No nothing.

"And my little nephew?"

"He left with his mom, he doesn't like Vivaldi," Carlos answered, sitting down again and looking at Héctor out of the corner of his eye.

"And you, what are you doing besides correcting books?" Héctor asked.

"I'll tell you only if you don't tell Marina."

"I swear."

"Swear on the Virgin of Guadalupe and the Jolly Green Giant combined."

"Come on, already."

"I'm involved in ideological warfare."

"Against whom?"

"Against a gang of juveniles. A bunch of guys from my neighborhood, the guys who spraypaint."

"What do they paint?"

"Bullshit," Carlos said, lighting a new cigarette. *"Sex Punks, Wild Border*—meaningless phrases like that, numbers, incomprehensible clues to mark their territory. It's like dog piss. Wherever I piss is my space and nobody can come in."

"And what do you do?"

"I paint on top of their paintings. I go out at night with my spray can and paint over theirs. It's war."

"But what do you paint?"

"Punks are Strawberries, Long Live Enver Hoxha, or *Che Guevara Lives, He's a Living Ghost, Be Careful Assholes, He Lives in the Neighborhood,* or *Sex Punks Were Born With a Silver Spoon in Their Mouths,* or *If a Dog Falls in the Water, Kick Him Until He Dies.* Some come out too long, they're not effective, but I hadn't painted in a long time; my da Vinci profusion is in arrears. I've got them screwed. It's not just ideological warfare; it's generational warfare, too. Obviously, it's a professional war and, in that, my painting technique dominates. Those sucklings are going to teach *me* how to paint walls . . . ? My most successful one was *Government = Punks Without Sneakers,* and the second most successful, celebrated to the hilt by the dry cleaner guy downstairs, had to do with a discount chain of stores. It was: *Paint Me a Blue Egg*

and Woolworth Will Buy It, but the Woolworth logo
didn't come out that well."

Héctor raised an eyebrow.

"Don't worry, it's not insanity, it's just to keep me in
shape until I find a new little place in the class war.
Besides, sometimes I agree with the punks and we
restore universal harmony. The other day I was painting one that said *If the PRI wants to govern, why don't
they start by winning the elections,* and the gang came
along and instead of destroying it, they wrote *Yes, that's
true* below it, six feet tall."

"And where is that painting?"

"Two blocks away. Want to go look at it?"

Héctor agreed. The morning was improving.

Detective Belascoarán Shayne firmly believed that
you cannot make friends after age thirty. That the im-
movable limit to construct and braid emotions within
that indestructible thing that is friendship is situated
one minute after age thirty; that after thirty there is a
certain emotional paralysis that impedes people from
risking themselves in the hazardous forming of the
passions of friendship. That after thirty, no one pricks
his finger and mixes his blood with others. But Héctor
had lost his great friends from before thirty and was
left with those from after. He had become someone
else after thirty and that other person was the one who
had made the new friends: his three office neighbors;
a radio journalist; a chubby female doctor; her brothers, two fighters; El Mago, his landlord . . . Héctor also

knew—if knowing is that absolute certainty that you acquire by dint of rethinking the same thing over and over again, and that old ladies call idiosyncrasies—that after thirty, a man cannot make friends with a woman. That there's too much pent-up sex wrapped up in the relationship, too much inopportune romanticism, too much fantasy between skirt and trousers for things to work. However, and to his utter surprise, when the woman opened the door, Héctor sensed that she could have been one of his best friends for the rest of his life had they met during childhood. This absurd certainty, so incongruous with the wisdom he had acquired, left him slightly stupefied.

The woman looked at him and gave a faint smile. Héctor looked at her with the face of someone studying the salami section in a gourmet deli. She looked behind her, as if expecting there to be someone back there to whom the detective was really directing that look of adoration and astonishment. There was no one. She came in and closed the door behind her, cautiously, not letting the fantasy escape her.

She was about thirty years old, with very dark, flowing hair, sparkling eyes, full lips, a turned-up nose; a scar about six or seven inches long on her neck, wide hips, and large breasts. She dressed as if the last ten years had passed in vain: a white blouse, a long black Indian skirt, boots, a very loose scarf not intended to cover the scar. She was smiling, always smiling.

"Héctor?"

"He went out to get something to drink. But you can tell me everything."

"Well then, who are you?"

"His secretary."

"What's going on?" she asked and searched for something in the giant knapsack hanging off her shoulder. The windows were open. Héctor was cold. It was December and the temperature went down in the afternoons. But it shouldn't have been that bad. The cold Héctor felt, the detective suspected, was in his blood; it came from his badly mended bones, it was the continuation of the same message of his dreams. Still, he walked, forcing himself to turn his back on the woman and what she had in her bag, and went to the window to close it.

"Let's see, is it or isn't it?" she asked, taking out a photograph and placing it on the desk. Héctor came back from the window, took out a cigarette, lit it. He picked up the photo and studied it.

The one on the right was Mendiola, the journalist; the one on the left was him, the other him from a couple of years ago. They were in the entrance of the Revolución Arena, after a wrestling match, mixed in among the exiting crowd. Their faces were surly, sullen, as if they had been the ones who had wrestled and failed, as if they'd respectively lost mask and hair in the duel and from the floor had been dished out two flying kicks to the balls. He didn't remember the moment or the picture, but he did remember the characters. Mendiola and Héctor Belascoarán Shayne, the other. The former.

He put the picture on the desk. The woman drew near, looked at the subject depicted and then compared it to the man in front of her.

"No, then they're not the same, are they? The one

in the photo looked better. You are more worn out, crippled, skinnier, one-eyed, mustached, the eye you have left lazy and half glazed-over, wiry muscles. But I like you more now despite the scrappiness. You seem fiercer, more of a bastard . . ."

"You're a pretty keen observer. What I see is I'm more tattered."

"Is that right?" She paused to study the room. "May I sit?"

"Even if I say no . . . My lady's name?"

"Not a lady's name, my name is Alicia. My sister used to say it was a hairdresser's name."

"And you wear contacts, your middle toe is longer than the others, and one breast looks to the left."

"There's no better description . . . I need a detective."

"They advertise in the Yellow Pages."

"I want this one," she said, pointing to Héctor.

"This one's retired, they retired him."

"And he doesn't take anything on? Easy things? Chaperoning sweet sixteen parties, serving as a bodyguard to a stupid singer, finding runaway cats, things like that . . . ?"

"Not even that. This one doesn't protect pets or sweet sixteen parties, he doesn't even take much care of himself. That you can see, Alicia."

"But can I talk to you or not?"

Héctor stood up, walked toward the safe, slapped the ass of a poster of Grace Renat and grabbed a Pepsi.

"Oh, my favorite drink."

Héctor stared at her. Hinting that he should allow her a Pepsi was a transgression he wouldn't have permitted his clientele even in the olden days, and these days, clientele didn't exist. The woman smiled at him. He took a second can out of the safe, carried them to the desk, and placed them beside the photo. The Héctor in the photo scowled at him. He moved one Pepsi over the character's face to avoid the static coming from the past, took his gun out of the holster under his arm, and started to open the can with the gunsight.

"I don't think I even have curiosity left," he said.

"Christ, they told me you'd tell me to go to hell, but I have a reckless faith, kid, reckless."

"Let's drink our Pepsi, then go."

"Where?"

"Each to her own, okay?"

"Listen, it's not okay, I've got a story to tell you. It's terrible, it's not a joke; I bring you an old picture of yourself, I smile at you until my lips go stiff and my teeth get cold, and nothing. Nothing?"

"Nothing," Héctor said. The pop top blew through the air. The phone rang.

"Héctor? It's Mendiola."

"I just saw a picture of you, friend. Why are you going around handing them out?"

"Is Alicia there?"

"I think so."

"Tell her yes, pal. Treat her well. She can be trusted."

"I went out to lunch," Héctor said and hung up. Then he stood up, hesitated. "I'll leave you to lock up when you finish your drink," he said to the woman.

He left, thinking that it wasn't just the fear of getting back into a character he no longer recognized as himself and who had the bad habit of walking around getting himself killed, it was also the terrible boredom of having to seem ingenious.

A gang of neighborhood teenagers was skateboarding in front of the door to his house. El Mago was watching with admiration from the door of the electronics store. It was getting dark. Héctor zipped up his jacket. He was cold. His right elbow and wrist ached. Arthritis? Swelling? Mexico City leprosy? He decided it was something simpler, a sign that he wanted double chicken soup with drumsticks and in a big bowl for dinner.

"Your girlfriend came by, she left a basket. I put it in your apartment," El Mago said, not looking away from the skateboarders making figure eights on the asphalt, wearing shabby electric-colored jackets, poor people's jackets, inherited from brothers who had outgrown them.

"What do you think, Mago, should I learn to repair televisions?" Héctor asked.

"Well, you've got to know something about electronics, right? That's what you studied. But I think it's too late, at your age, you don't have the grace of a ballerina with your hand on the trigger, which is what the job requires."

"That's what I thought. Looking at you, that's what I thought."

El Mago detached his gaze from the skaters and looked at Héctor.

"Wipe that look off your face, kid, you're making me

sick," he said and turned back to the boys, to one in particular, who let a little cardboard box fall on the ground, then distanced himself and rapidly propelled himself toward it, bent over and brushed it with his hair, doubling over, then leaped and got vertical again.

"Do you think that at my age I could be a good detective?" El Mago asked, hoping to take Héctor by surprise.

"No," Héctor answered, lighting a cigarette and inhaling deeply. "You lack the grace to draw a gun without catching the barrel on your fly and blowing your balls off."

"That's what I said, shithead. Ever since Franco died, life no longer offers any new sensations. The best thing that happens to me is having you as a tenant and that every once in a while a few guys come along and scare the shit out of you by shooting out your windows."

Héctor slapped El Mago on the back and went inside the building. There were a couple of letters on the first step of the staircase: one a flyer from American Express that he left there, and the other his bank statement, which he opened as he went up the stairs. Counting everything plus inflation, he had enough cash for one year without having to ask Elisa for any of the money they'd inherited from their father. He knew that, but he looked at the numbers carefully so he could repeat them cent for cent the next time somebody offered him work.

The basket was in the middle of the living room rug. A bright red rug in a room with no furniture. It was a shopping basket that contained two yellowish ducks no taller than ten inches, and a card. The ducks were ardently saying quack, quack, quack, the envelope was labeled with a simple *For you.*

The note was laconic, like everything about her:

> *I took a photo shoot in Puerto Vallarta. Two weeks. I hope your mood has passed by the time I get home. The gentlemen are called Octavio Paz and Juan José Arreola. A hug. They eat birdseed and hard bread twice a day, they drink water all the time. If they shit on your shirt, you can start praying for Francesca Dry Cleaning to reopen.*
>
> *Me.*

Héctor contemplated the tiny little ducks with their yellowish, silly faces. They reminded him of a rabbit called Rataplán that once roamed the apartment. The woman with the ponytail believed that Héctor became dangerous in solitude and every time she left, she tried to leave something for company: a portrait, two ducks, a long tape with just one song on it, a rabbit, a stuffed roasted turkey and an electric knife to slice it, the complete works of Dashiell Hammett in twelve volumes.

That was the way it was.

He contemplated the ducks' maneuvers on the rug, he walked over to the record player and put on Silvio Rodríguez's latest. Side A, track three. He peered out the window, the skateboarders had gone. The sound of the chains that made the metal gate go down told him that El Mago was closing the store.

You have to love the hour that never shines. And

don't, don't pretend to pass the time, only love engenders wonder. Only love can wake the dead.

He'd been playing the same song for a month. Curiously, he wasn't learning the words, though he enjoyed all of them in bits each time. But love wasn't waking anything. It didn't light up more than a few hours, a few minutes and always in the solitude of two. It didn't shed more than ten square feet of occasional light. He went back to the window trying not to step on the ducks erratically circling around the rug. The streetlights turned on as if desire had created a magical order.

After all, it wasn't that bad, the story didn't make for a tragedy. It was just a guy covered with scars who was scared. And the fear wasn't that bad, it was good company, as rational as love or ducks or the cold. He walked to his room and came back with a black wool vest, stopped in the kitchen and filled a little plate with water for the ducks. He watched them drink. Such pigs, they walked in and out of the plate, shat in it, drank and splashed; the water was clouding over and the rug around the plate getting soaked. It was a good rug. Red. Here and there there were a few stains—wine stains, swallow's nest soup, acid from a Volkswagen battery, other people's blood. He walked over to the record player again and put the needle back in the groove of track three. One of the ducks had discovered the joys of diving and he leaned against the edge of the plate to fling himself onto the rug and then staggered a little. That had to be JJ. He tried to differentiate him from the other one. He had a coffee stain on his wing. OP had a sly look and a circle of white down on his head. Now the phone is going to ring, Héctor said to himself. Out of the speakers came: *You should love yourself to insanity. Only love lights what lasts.* Now, he thought, the phone is going to ring, counting one, two ... and ... three. But nothing rang and Héctor went back to the kitchen to make a tortilla with potatoes and Michoacán sausages according to old man Belascoarán's recipe. OP and JJ would adore the tortilla. Either that or they would face starvation.

The city that one possesses is not the one that others have. The one one has, one's own, has the lampposts in the wrong place, it fills with shadows where there shouldn't be any. In the one one has, the newspaper seller displays *Ovaciones* folded over so that one has to perform miracles in order to read the ninety-point headline, and even then just barely. In one's own city, the corner store invariably closes at 7:15 even though when one asks them in the morning what time they'll be closing that night, they say 8:00; in one's city, Channel 9 has static when they run the Bogart movies. The personal city may have a kinship with the other cities: misery, unemployment, the unreliability of the electrical power, the price of gas, the black cloud of smog that travels northwest to southwest, the ill humor of the fifth-floor neighbors, the standard taste of the hamburgers in fast-food joints, the cleaning lady's instantaneous reaction when a lamp suddenly shudders, announcing an earthquake. But that's decoration. We experience different cities, linked by the abuses of power and fear, corruption, and the eternal threat of descent into the jungle, that hides in the system; it pops up regularly to remind us that we are fragile, that we are alone, that one day we will be fodder for the buzzards. Or that one day, all will have to be risked at once, Western style, Main Street shoot-out style: them or us.

Faced with this solitude, one's own city creates its sympathies, tepid dams made of toothpicks that occasionally resist the spate of the flood. The smile of the clerk in the paint shop; the wink of casual complicity on the bus with the guy who's reading the same novel; the complacency of the subway passengers before the cannibalistic kiss with which two students part company, as if there won't be classes again tomorrow; the hostile look shared by the passersby before the corner cop who is chewing out a motorcyclist. And inside one's own city, other cities are made, smaller towns, almost private ranches that connect every once in a while with other people's cities.

Which city did I live in this last year? Héctor Belascoarán Shayne, retired detective, asked himself. Who did I live with? Who else did I live with these last twelve months? He couldn't really remember. A lot of hospital images. A vacation in someone's house in the mountains near Puebla, surrounded by pine trees. A doctor who insisted on the healing benefits of forest air for lung injuries. An unpaid bill for four liters of blood plasma. A Puma soccer game in the CU stadium with Carlos Vargas, El Gallo, and Gilberto as cheerleading, grandstand, and beer-drinking companions. A job re-

constructing a village aqueduct in the state of Queré-
taro. Two books by Jean-François Vilar and the late
discovery of Pío Barojas's social novels. A casual, sweaty
relationship, lasting six days, with a redheaded bio-
chemistry student. An entire year. Not much to justify
a year. And things had happened in the country. He
had a vague notion that the populace was getting nervous, their irritation was taking form, that Mexicans
were walking around singing the national anthem:
when that happened, Héctor's historic memory thought
it recalled, it was usually a warning of a great storm.

The elevator creaked up to the office as Héctor was
trying uselessly to recover the last year of his life. The
elevator door opened before it should have. Alicia gave
him a lavish smile and entered without his being able
to stop her. She pushed the sixth-floor button.

"Alicia, remember?" she said.

"No, I'm not Alicia. I'm a retiree going to the third
floor. More than two floors of stoppage against my will
can technically be considered an abduction," he said
and looked down at the elevator floor.

"Damn it," the woman said.

Héctor looked at her.

Alicia was wearing a sweater and black wool pants.
She grabbed her sweater at the waist and slowly lifted
it to expose her breasts to the open air. She wasn't
wearing a bra. They were bigger than they suggested
when covered. Pointed, with pink nipples.

"It's true, one is bigger than the other . . . In addition
to the abduction, rape . . ."

She put her sweater back where it belonged. Héctor
felt dejected. It was like wearing a muzzle. Didn't they

say the mouth was faster than the brain? The door opened onto the sixth floor. Defeated, Alicia pressed the third floor.

"It's okay, I give up," Héctor said. "I'm listening."

II

The Story of Luke Estrella as Told by Alicia
(Just as Héctor Belascoarán would later
remember it)

He killed her, I know he killed her. But it couldn't have been him. He wasn't inside the bathroom, she had locked herself in. It wasn't with his hands, it's not that he pulled the trigger. He killed her another way, and of that I'm sure, because I know he killed her. He was pushing her down a damned dead-end street, at the end of it was the bathroom with the door locked from the inside and the revolver, and she was sitting on the toilet with her brains smeared across the wall, while the neighbors knocked on the door and a tape recorder in the apartment was playing Manzanero music. That's how she had to die, to Manzanero music. She was always listening to sugary boleros, you know? Toward the end, she listened to those boleros all day, all the time. She and the tape player walked the house together, while he was pushing her down the hall, sometimes yelling, sometimes with a kitchen knife telling her to take off her clothes so that a few friends who'd come over for dinner could see her naked.

When I was in Miami in April, three years ago, she told me that she had moved their twin beds as far apart as she could. But every night he pushed them a little closer together. That time she showed me the burns on her arm that he had made with an iron because she didn't want to try cocaine. And it ended in that, too. The autopsy said she was drugged up to her ears, to the marrow of her bones. But how could that be, if before the most she ever took was Pepsi Light, for the caffeine. How was she going to be on drugs if she never even took two aspirin at a time, one at the most if her head ached too much. That prick, that son of the cunt of his mother, son of a fucking bitch, faggot. That guy would get high and turn red from all the shit he put up his nose, injected into his veins, and then he'd think himself a man and his dick wouldn't work for shit. How could foolish Elena go and marry a wretch like that? My sister was naive, she was an absolute idiot. Because the guy was handsome, Luke Estrella, the handsome rumba dancer, the charmer. In the beginning he even convinced me with all his turns of phrase, showing off his muscles under his clingy T-shirt, showing off his balls with his fitted jeans, and showing off his dollars and the red sports car that had cost him eight thousand bills right here, right now, old lady, and here it is for you to try out, and my sister, the fool, letting herself fall, drooling over her golden mulatto who would take her away from eight hours in the office and would take her to Hollywood, and instead of that pure bullshit, he gave her sixteen in hell and eight in damn purgatory.

He killed her. He was pushing her toward insanity and no doubt saying, *Don't you dare? Kill yourself. I bet you don't have the guts.* She wrote me a letter—I don't have it anymore, I threw it out; the letter went to hell all full of tears, all snotty from my crying— where she told me that he once made her crawl on her knees through the house while he threatened her with a gun. Because that's how that son of a bitch really was. One day he'd take her to a fancy restaurant to dine over French wine and the next day he'd take her credit card so she couldn't use it while he was away. One day he'd cry in front of her and tell her he'd never loved anyone so much and the next he'd introduce her to his boss in a bar and leave her there so the other could take her to bed. He was a shiteater, that guy. A sick rat. Elena told me once he was poisoning her with cockroach-killing powder, and then she told me he wasn't, that he was putting sugar in the cockroach envelopes so she would think he was poisoning her. He wanted to kill her in the head, drive her crazy. He threatened to shoot her if she tried to escape, then he would disappear for weeks, but some gringo would call her every day on his behalf, asking her if she needed anything.

Elena left the only way she could leave, blowing her brains out. And he must have been quite content because the only thing that mattered to that shit-crazy pig was power. To have her enslaved, to control her so much, so much that one day he could kill her to prove how much she was his, how much he had her. Luke Estrella, the very proud widower, so radiant in his black silk suit, shiny patent leather shoes, little white vest, the asshole who is on his way to Mexico.

You've got to fuck him up, for me. He's coming to Mexico next week. I'm sure, he's arriving on Pan Am's

Thursday night flight. Pan Am from New York. I work for an airline and I asked all my friends to tell me if his name came up on the computer. He's got a reservation to come to Mexico on Thursday and no doubt he's coming to pull some kind of shit, because that's the only thing he knows how to do. Up there in Miami, he was always involved in strange things, in drugs, I think, and that shit, with the Cuban mafia in Miami, the *gusanos*, the guys who owned the neighborhood. And so you have to find out what it is and you have to bring him down, so they can grab him and he can rot in some Mexican jail, forever, to pay for what he did to Elena. Look, here's a photo, look at him, so smiley, the big asshole, as if he were saying *Nobody touches me.* Forty-five years old, he was older than my sister when they got married. So you can, can't you? You're going to fuck him good, right? There is justice and that son of a bitch is going to die in a Mexican jail, right? Isn't that right . . . ?

III

My scars have roots even in other bodies, my wounds move in shame.

Roque Dalton

"And what did you tell her?" Héctor asked.

"What the hell was I going to tell her?" an indignant Gilberto Gómez Letras said.

"Well, I don't know, something about common sense."

"Shit, yes. I said didn't it seem stupid to her to change the entire installation instead of just changing the knobs that said hot and cold."

"Well, yes, and what did she say?"

"That ever since she was a little girl, she'd gotten used to the hot being on the right and the cold on the left, and that's the way she wanted it. Note, stupid Héctor, the stupid dense people one has to deal with every day. At this point, I'd like to shoot myself like one of your lowlifes, those guys who rape worn-out women, those idiots who stick a .45 up their ass then fire. As a murderer and an annoyance, the old lady is tops."

Gómez Letras considered the conversation over and concentrated on an eight-foot length of copper tubing that he was whipping around the office from side to side, skipping over desks and chairs.

Héctor had stolen two packets of sugar from a coffee shop and was trying to improve his Coke, pouring them in along with half a lime. As far as flavor went, the result of the experiment was open to discussion, but quite a nice frothy foam welled up. In the club across the street, they'd spent half the morning playing the same second-rate tropical record, the kind that pounds the rhythm and lacks a melody; he hadn't been able to pick up much of the words except that they were talking about a mulatto woman with a green ribbon in her hair.

Gómez Letras was smiling as he worked the copper tube to the rhythm of the tropical piece. His bad mood seemed to have dissolved.

"Why are you laughing?"

"I was thinking that if we stick a .45 up that woman's ass, she might not give a shit which side the hot water is on."

"Better let your evil thoughts die there."

"Did you see that they raised the price of soda?"

"It's already common knowledge that in this city we all walk around with a .45 up our ass."

"Hand me those tweezers."

"I'm going to hand you a .45 so you can see what it feels like."

"I feel better, but you must be exhausted by now ... And speaking of that, how *do* you feel?"

"I don't know, let me think about it," Héctor said.

He walked to the window and took a long swig of his improved Coke.

"Bad, I think I feel bad."

"Well, it's about time to start feeling better, there's not much action around here."

"What do you know about Afghanistan?"

"Nothing, it's a street in the El Rosario neighborhood, isn't it? What's going on over there?"

"The KGB is looking for Mexican plumbers."

"The KGB is a water pump factory in León, Guanajuato, right?"

Now it was Héctor's turn to smile. Gómez Letras looked at him, annoyed. He moved to counterattack.

"You call yourself the poor people's detective, but you haven't even been to the protests."

"The students?"

"No shit."

"Like the little rat in the story said . . ."

"What did he say?"

"I've been sick."

"And whoever shits on the record player, pees on it, puts his feet on top of it, splashes water, or coughs up chewed corn, I'll wring his neck and roast him," Héctor said to JJ and OP, showing them the John Coltrane cover again, the one with "Stardust." The ducks emitted a string of quack-quacks and disappeared into the kitchen wagging their tails.

Héctor turned on the record player, removed the fluff from the needle and took the Coltrane out of its slip; he took off his jacket and turned on every light in the house. It was a new habit developed over these last few months. He was seeking the sensation of being the center of a Christmas tree where the light warded off all fears. He set down the needle and turned up the volume on both speakers. Then he went into the bathroom and pissed peacefully. The two photographs Alicia had given him were pinned to the wall above the toilet. He had them there to get used to during the week prior to the man's arrival in the Mexico City airport, prior to the encounter with Luke Estrella's actual face. For now, just the photos: a light-skinned mulatto, slightly split jaw, round nose, dry eyes, broad forehead. The Hollywood Latin mustache, soft, uneven.

Héctor spun around to the mirror as he shook off and studied his own mustache—rough, chaotic, Pancho Villa style.

Now he began a history of mustaches and Héctor knew well that tomorrow would be a day of a long-distance runner in training, of reading a book by Lansford about Pancho Villa and the North Division (his latest spiritual guide), of going to Gate E of Benito Juárez Airport and choosing the column from behind which to observe, the store to buy a drink, the parking lots, the place to leave the car. What a joke . . . mustaches.

The thing was working, he said to himself. He went down the hall to the kitchen and left the revolver next to the .45 automatic. He stuck everything including the holster in the refrigerator. The thing was working. Well oiled: the ducks, "Stardust," the lights; all the medicine against loneliness he'd been able to gather.

*   *   *

The doorbell rang. It was still night. Gray, black dawn was almost breaking. It was the buzzer on the downstairs door. Héctor tried to fix his pajama bottoms, which had almost fallen off during his nocturnal nightmares. He was drenched with sweat. Again, the sweats, the taste of dirt in his mouth, bitter dirt. Fucking again. He peered out the window, hobbling, because he'd stubbed his toes on the base of the sink. Carlos, his brother, wrapped in a black jacket, stood under the streetlight. Héctor felt the cold.

"Come down," Carlos said.

"You come up."

"No, come down and let's go."

"Where?"

"To the campus."

Dawn broke decisively as they crossed San Antonio on Revolución, in the midst of a fog that Héctor charitably classified as natural, but that Carlos identified as definitely part of the industrial shit; the black cloud of smog that traveled north to south utilizing the viaduct of the Beltway and Revolución Avenue, pushed by malignant winds whose function was to disperse the pollution and provide cover for the ghost of James Dean who rode around on his motorcycle in those parts.

The mist made the profile of buildings and trees a hundred yards away look diffuse, phantasmal.

"Are you carrying a gun?"

"Two, you want one? They're half frozen because I kept them in the fridge last night."

Carlos laughed. He shook his head no. "No way, armed and I shoot myself . . . No, I asked so that you don't even think about using them."

"What? Do I look like the Lone Ranger? I don't go around firing off shots," Héctor said and then asked, "Why are we going?"

"I hear they're trying to break up the CEU strike, the student strike."

"Who?"

"The police, the right-wing groups, the university president's dogs."

Héctor stayed quiet. Yes, it had to be pollution, because his only healthy eye was watering. He should have felt honored by Carlos choosing him as his traveling companion. In other words, the best thing to do was shut up and smile. No asking if they weren't a little old to go around defending a student strike that for fifteen days had been abusing a city which the earthquake, the economic crisis, and disappointment seemed to have exhausted, and that was now rising up again: trembling, adolescent, shouting, reborn.

Traffic cleared out on the access road to the university. Hector felt one brief pang of nostalgia and two of fear. After all, it was his university. Or was it? It was as much his as the rest of the country's; it wasn't a housing development belonging to an authoritarian administration with the mentality of a supermarket owner. And anyway, it was as good a return to life as any other.

Carlos had remained silent. He drove the Volkswagen with a kind of professional cold dexterity, always looking ahead, both hands on the steering wheel.

"How long has it been since you've been to the university?" Héctor asked.

"About ten years. I think the last time was when I stopped by the Philosophy Film Club to see Fellini's

8½ again. Too much nostalgia at once. I didn't like the movie as much as I had before. I left the university like a prisoner just released, hiding, so no ghost would recognize me."

"And me not even that much," Héctor said as he felt his hands starting to sweat. Damned biological, physical fear, stuck in his bones. Would it never disappear?

The first barricades were next to the gas station. A few barrels of oil were burning, making small black clouds. The stupid students these days were not ecologists. Some five thousand of them had gathered around that entrance to the campus. You couldn't see any cops around. Carlos, a member of the old and wary left, of the generation that learned to distrust invisible cops, drove around the nearby streets a couple of times. A truck with riot police about ten blocks away, two patrol cars on Copilco, nothing out of the ordinary. They parked in front of the Technical Library and approached the action on foot. A bunch of guys were singing with a couple of guitars. It wasn't the "We Will Triumph" of Quilapayún or a song from Atahualpa Yupanqui or "The Girl from Guatemala" by José Martí-Oscar Chávez; yet the nostalgia was there in the Beatles' "Let It Be." This generation, thought Héctor— looking around at the ponchos and the budding beards, the blue and gold sweaters, light jackets, skirts longer than ever—was like him: it had never found its moment of glory. Not yet, anyway, he said to himself. He walked over to one of the oil barrels to dry the sweat off his hands. He couldn't shake the fear, but at least he would accompany the five thousand students with the best of brave appearances. It was the least he could do for them.

The guitarists and the chorus finished "Let It Be" and someone started singing a Benedetti poem. The police who were going to break up the strike never showed.

"Does life smile at you?" Héctor asked Gómez Letras a few hours later, while Gómez Letras toiled at installing a new bathtub in his house.

"Me, life fights me," the plumber and officemate said indifferently.

"Do you object to philosophy?" Héctor asked, looking around and tearing because the cigarette smoke had gotten in his eye.

The plumber contemplated him carefully. He had his doubts, especially over these last few weeks, about the quality of the detective's mental state. When he saw that the weeping was going no further and had to do with the puff of smoke, he calmed down but he didn't feel obliged to answer.

"Do you believe in luck?" Héctor insisted, asking almost out of inertia, because he couldn't think of anything better to do.

"I believe other people have luck."

"Do you think women and men are equal?"

"It depends on how you arrange them."

"Have you ever gotten laid by a Christian?"

"I think I was really drunk once and I screwed a Mormon. But I didn't mean to, so it doesn't count."

"Do you already know who you're going to vote for?"

"Shit yeah, Cárdenas."

"But weren't you an abstentionist?"

"That was before. Now, yes, we should screw the PRI."

"Who's we?"

"The Cárdenas people. Where have you been, boss?"

Héctor couldn't think of any more questions, nor did he think it was worth the trouble to answer, and he went off smoking down the hall, leaving Gómez Letras to work on the bathtub. The afternoon light was waning.

"I'm leaving. Make yourself at home," he yelled from the front door.

Gómez Letras peered out to watch him leave, still a little worried. Héctor almost tripped over the ducks.

"Stay in the shadows, boss, you're acting pretty dopey."

He hopped down the steps, thinking about the bathtub.

The bathtub was being installed for free, thanks to a bet. Héctor had wagered that the university team would score against Atlante and the plumber, momentarily weak, had allowed his populist whims to influence him. Now he was installing a bathtub, free of charge, in the detective's house, even though it had cost him a little extra to buy the materials. Héctor wanted a bathtub. If the plumber was feeling nostalgic for the lower class and bet on the mangiest team in the first division of Mexican soccer, Héctor couldn't give a shit. Since his earliest childhood, the scene of voluptuous

Cleopatra soaking herself was fixed in his memory, and he dreamed shamefully of having gardenia salt baths. When death loomed very near, or the sensation of death came visiting, inhibitions were lost, fear of the ridiculous evaporated, the prudish barriers crumbled, and the silliest taboos managed to die, allowing the phantoms to peer out from under the bed. With gardenias, just like an Australian whore, he said to himself, smiling, mocking himself.

The afternoon light had vanished by the time he got down the stairs. Only neon and mercury lit his way to the taxi stand. It was only eight at night, but the street was surprisingly empty. Somewhere a record player replete with rancheras was howling at the moon like an urban coyote. It was a good night. Cold air you could almost taste. A wind from the south, from the eternal winter winds of El Ajusco, just enough to rouse the skin, briefly bristle the down, sensitizing the poorly shaved chin, clearing the color of the eyes (the eye). Héctor accelerated his pace, not straying outside the lit area, looking behind him every once in a while. He was less afraid now than other nights, but habits stick to the cerebral cortex of the brain, the rituals of fear repeat themselves and bring back terrors by doing so.

At Insurgentes Square, he went into the subway. The train had a few empty seats. He took a novel by Marc Behm out of his coat pocket and vanished inside it. He emerged from the pages of the book half a dozen stops later, at Isabel la Católica, and got off the orange train. He walked a dozen blocks to the Hotel Luna. Not many people on the streets. It was the Thursday before payday, people locked themselves in to share their economic woes with the television. It was cold.

He checked into the hotel under the name of Arturo Cane, travel agent, and they put him in Room 111. He took stock of the small bathroom, washed his hands, took off his coat, and fell onto the bed. He resumed his reading. Half an hour later he realized his eye hadn't moved off the same line. What had he been thinking about? The revolver in the holster was making his ribs hurt a little, still he didn't take it off; he closed his eye and tried to convince himself he was sleeping. He managed.

The light woke him up gradually and this time he didn't come out of a nightmare, just a gray cloud in which Chopin was playing. He remembered a particularly unpleasant flu from his childhood and the experiment of Chopin as a cure for the fever that his mother had devised. It hadn't worked, but Chopin was incontrovertibly linked in his memory to a 104 degree temperature, muscle aches, and cold sweats.

He did not wake up wondering where he was. He was in a hotel room. He had done it again. As he hoisted himself out of bed, Héctor seriously considered the possibility of committing himself to a mental asylum, of buying a ticket to heaven with the family psychiatrist. What was this shit about sleeping in hotels, registering under false names? Who was the idiot inside his head toying with his fears?

He had read in a novel that a paranoid could be defined as a Mexico City citizen with an acute perception of reality and an abundance of common sense. It was a funny joke, but this was going a little far. Okay, fine, peeing during nightmares was good. Crying in the street upon seeing a beggar was even better: it was a healthier reaction than walking right by him pretending he didn't exist. Packing two guns and a knife, fine, fucking fine, not a big deal, apart from the fact that he was carrying three pounds of excess equipment, looking over his shoulders even in the movies, hearing footsteps in the hallway, doubting the integrity of the milkman or the identity of the gas man, fine, perfect, very healthy. But sleeping in hotels under assumed names, calling a revolting aunt whom he hadn't seen for twenty years to cry as he told her some tearful story just because she was the closest thing to a mother figure he could pull out of his memory, that was too much already. That was too much shit already. Who was ordering him to go into a hotel? When did he decide?

Héctor threw off the clothes he'd slept in. He made himself stand in front of the mirror, studied his naked body carefully, the tons of scars collected over his early years, the tremendous bags under his eyes, the grayish paleness, the fear in his healthy eye, the lamentable scar where his other eye should have been. He forced a smile, then another wider one.

For the next hour, Belascoarán Shayne, Mexican detective, tried out thousands of smiles in front of the mirror. Then he washed his face with cold water, put over his eye a black leather patch that matched his jacket and got dressed.

He would have to learn to live with himself.

* * *

The New York–Washington–Mexico City Pan Am flight had just landed. That gave him fifteen minutes while the passengers went through immigration and customs. The airport was strangely deserted. It wasn't the time, maybe it was the day. Or maybe it was him, smelling like death and therefore repelling crowds. Or the city, which frightened tourists with those caved-in buildings from the earthquake that hid the bodies, and whose silhouettes surrounded by dust-filled air and by bare-chested, anonymous heroes had danced on the TV screens of a hundred thousand other cities, jerking brotherly tears here and there. But brotherly tears don't do much for tourism, and the memory is short, Héctor said to himself. He quickly looked for one of the little shops and got himself a Coke in an aluminum can, the kind of can that after drinking you can squash, and can transport the actor of the deed to the paradise of Hollywood stuntmen. He looked at a few boys who were porters playing hopscotch on the polished, shiny floor.

The electronic screen fascinated him for a couple of minutes. He was missing out on a lot of places, there were thousands of trips to take. And thousands of returns to the city of miracles, the city of horrors. Calling Mexico City "the monster" had become very vogue, but the nickname hid the better definition. He preferred to speak of his city as the cave of lies, the cavern of cannibals, the city of prostitutes on bicycles or in the black car of a cabinet minister, the cemetery of talking TVs, the city of men looking over their shoulders at their pursuers, the village occupied by label counterfeiters, the paradise of press conferences, the collapsed city, trembling, lovingly in ruins, its debris rummaged through by the moles of God.

In his decalogue on mystery novels, Chandler forgot to prohibit detectives from getting metaphysical, Héctor Belascoarán Shayne—gun-carrying argonaut of Mexico City, the world's biggest city at its own expense, the biggest cemetery of dreams—said to himself.

When he recognized Luke Estrella, a sensation of unreality invaded him. It is a lie that one recognizes people after having looked at their picture a hundred times. The illusion that the whole thing was a game vanished. The guy was there, dragging a black leather suitcase on wheels, sunglasses as dark as death, white patent leather shoes, black pants made from a synthetic nylon that shone with the reflections of the neon lights in the international wing of the airport. Shit, Héctor said to himself, almost regretting having spotted Luke Estrella, who, not knowing he'd been targeted by the astonished gaze of the detective, went on dodging two porters and two little blond girls who were hugging each other and crying under their mother's long legs.

Estrella was like his photo, but aged, his curly hair was streaked with gray hairs, his lips were thicker and drooping, perhaps in a wince of exhaustion; a tropical sway probably learned in the prostitute bars of Miami, a partially dark grimace in the corner of his mouth, a walk without brushing against anyone, above and distanced from the sparse crowd waiting to divest the relative just in from New York of the booty from the gift shops of Manhattan.

Héctor didn't know what to do, he had not anticipated Estrella's materialization in spite of his previous good intentions, he couldn't quite believe that the guy would appear so unruffled, so alive, in the middle of the night in Mexico City. Estrella dragged his suitcase toward the taxi stand door. Héctor saw him pass practically at his side, brushing against him. Then he reacted and ran out to the tower parking lot. With the first steps of the race the realization came: if he rented a car now, he would never be able to find the *gusano*. He turned around, reentered the terminal, used the same exit Estrella had. The Cuban was waiting in line, Héctor lined up two places behind him, with a fat German lady between them.

"How much to the Hotel Presidente, kiddo?" Estrella asked into the little window.

Héctor smiled. Detectives, like soccer goalies, have fifty-five percent luck and the rest natural talent to hurl themselves into the appropriate spot.

He entered a cab in his turn, rode calmly through the viaduct. The city was emptier than usual, lonelier, sadder. Passing through Monterrey and the neighborhood of Los Doctores, you could make out the ruins three hundred feet away. Hector thought about the distance. He needed to back off. He'd approached Estrella twice. A one-eyed man is exceedingly visible, like a brand of cola on a television ad, you always get the feeling you've seen him before. The only thing he was missing was a fluorescent T-shirt and a couple of rumba dancers hanging off his arm. He would have to get the glass eye out of the dresser drawer, he would have to put on a no-man's-face, he'd have to dress like a lamppost, anonymous, like an ad for something out of style, he would have to follow Estrella from a distance if he wanted to fuck him.

And he did.

IV

The most fascinating quality about things is that they change so quickly that one keeps thinking of them the way they were before.

Paco Ignacio Taibo I

Héctor knew from past experience that creatively tailing someone requires double the hours that the guy invests in getting around. Because you have to touch what the guy touches, you have to go back over his steps to find out what size shoe the man wears who crossed paths with him on the terrace; what he spoke about with the pale blonde, and who she sleeps with; the name of the waiter and how much the bill was. If you didn't work like that, the whole thing turned into a silent movie, indecipherable, because the actors are usually bad, weak, always veering from the already incomprehensible script. It was either that, or technology: to close the distance with telephoto lenses and wireless microphones placed on the tail of a cat or the neckline of a trapeze artist swinging between the lamps.

Resolve the contradiction, he said to himself. Approach fully or back off and return two or three times over the guy's tracks. Héctor was eclectic and didn't have access to technology beyond a pair of rubber sandals that didn't squeak.

That's why the first day was a failure.

Luke Estrella moved through Mexico City without much hesitancy, including knowing a few codes that are usually reserved for natives and denied to tourists, like not hailing the taxi in front of the hotel, but walking a couple of blocks and stopping one as it passed, which would certainly be cheaper; like wrapping your big bills inside smaller ones; like you don't need coins for the public phones because even though the instructions order you to insert one, after the earthquake the phone company disconnected the payment system due to the emergency situation and it's still that way. Estrella hardly even paused before crossing the streets, he didn't make unnecessary turns. This guy knew Mexico City; what's more, he had been here within the last year. He didn't look at the crumbled buildings from the earthquake with any particular interest, he wasn't interested in the park plaza fire-eaters, he wasn't surprised by the street booksellers.

After a peaceful, solitary night in the hotel (he even ate in his room, a suite on the sixteenth floor), Estrella had spent the day in a dance without much meaning around the streets in the center of Mexico City: a visit to Aurora Jewelry on Alameda, from which he exited without having bought a thing; a long walk up and down San Juan de Letrán, ending in the purchase of a couple of postcards in the post office, which he filled out right there, put the stamps on and deposited in one of the mailboxes (air mail/international); he went up to the top floor of the Latin American Tower and spent half an hour contemplating the artificial gray fog that covered the city from the southwest to the north.

Later, another walk toward Mexico City's minuscule Chinatown, down narrow Dolores Street. He ate there in a mediocre restaurant where even the waiters were Mandarin. The woman at the table next to him, a plain blonde about forty-five years old, made a little conversation with him, but Héctor, three tables away, couldn't pick up anything of importance, beyond Estrella's blowing her off, after a few polite smiles. The Cuban-American spent two hours in the afternoon in a shoe store buying boots. Three pairs, one of them very expensive crocodile leather, which he had sent to the hotel, and later he sat down to read the papers in the Alameda, his back to the statue of Benito Juárez. When it started getting dark, he went back to the hotel and did not reappear.

Estrella had spent his day blissfully and Héctor felt like an idiot.

Too innocent to be true. Either he was waiting for a contact, or someone was helping him figure out if he was being tailed; if that were the case, Héctor could have been easily identified; he had taken no precautions other than concealing himself from the Cuban.

Around twelve at night, Belascoarán dropped into the hardest armchair in his office, the one in which he couldn't fall asleep due to the springs that stuck out and jutted into his butt, and he decided he didn't like Luke Estrella one bit, but he didn't like Héctor Belascoarán Shayne much either.

Estrella, if what Alicia had told him were true, was a son of a bitch. If he'd never heard the story, he would have known it just from seeing the way he walked through the city without touching it, without letting it touch him, the way he looked at things with no affection; he smiled too much, he couldn't spare a friendly look for the people selling single Kleenexes. Estrella was minding his own business, Estrella was waiting, Estrella was killing time. And Héctor, who knew a lot about death, felt betrayed after a day of useless pursuit.

If a detective orthodoxy happens to exist, a heterodoxy must also exist, a kind of heresy. That is why, after his tenth filtered Delicado, Héctor Belascoarán Shayne got up from the armchair with the popped springs, and at about three in the morning went back out again, stopped a taxi in front of the door to his office, and asked to be taken to the Hotel Presidente Chapultepec.

He registered as Manuel Lombadero, native of Barcelona, paying with American Express traveler's checks that he had countersigned and that he couldn't remember how had gotten into his coat pocket. Maybe he'd put them there during one of his many paranoid ravings and signed that strange name, which he recognized as the production assistant of a Spanish mystery movie. Life was already sufficiently bizarre and he was insisting on making it still more grotesque. The reception manager swallowed the tried-and-true excuse that he'd lost his luggage in the airport and Héctor let himself be led to a room on the sixteenth floor, three doors down from Estrella's.

Once he was alone, Héctor carefully checked the bathroom and terrace, turned on the TV to a station broadcasting pure static, and fell asleep without undressing.

He never found out whether what woke him was his gun driving into his ribs, the start of the morning programming on Channel 13 (whose slogan had been touched up by Carlos Vargas: *It's already morning/to Channel 13 I'm turning/the more I see/the more it grows on me*), or destiny. He'd slept three or four hours and was inundated by that feeling of unreality produced by exhaustion.

He heard muffled screams in the hallway. Héctor poked his head out cautiously and saw a bleeding man reaching his arms out to him. A persecuted man recognizes the look of fear in other faces; that might be why, without thinking about it, Héctor extended a hand toward the man and tugged at him to pull him inside the room. He kicked the door shut without stopping to look if anyone was coming after this bloody character.

The guy fell on his knees, looked at Héctor, and, through the fog of the blood that covered his left eye and trickled down his face to his chin, tried to form a faint smile.

"Hello, I am Dick," he stammered, in English.

"I'm not," said Héctor, who had always wanted to start a dialogue that way, with the absolute worst timing, as in every crime movie he'd ever seen.

The man rolled over slowly and remained on the floor, calmly staining the dark blue rug with his blood.

There were two dry knocks on the door behind the detective. Héctor turned mechanically and opened again. Before him stood Estrella, draped in silk pajamas.

"Pardon me, sir, an associate of mine had an accident, hurt himself; you see, he was a little drunk, out of it, you say here . . ." Estrella said as he tried to enter. He didn't meet the detective's eye.

Héctor placed himself between the door and the fallen gringo, but Luke Estrella had penetrated the room enough to see him.

"What happened to him . . . ?"

"No one has entered this room," Héctor said, "aside from that friend of mine who is sleeping on the rug."

"The joke . . ."

Héctor drew his .45, cocked it, and pressed it against the Cuban's forehead.

"And furthermore, my friend doesn't like to have his sleep disturbed."

"Sorry to bother you," Estrella said, retreating; then he stared at Héctor as if wanting to memorize his face. A good dose of hatred in the eyes, Héctor thought as he closed the door. A small shiver ran up his spine.

The gringo tried to get up, but reeled and landed back flat with his head on the rug.

The best place to hold a business meeting: Chapultepec Lake. The center of the lake to be exact. Rowing between the contaminated swans, which increasingly grow to resemble the faces of Treasury Department functionaries on the verge of retiring. Possible on a gray day, impossible on a sunny day like that one.

Héctor had left the hotel carrying the gringo on his shoulders down a freight elevator, surrounded by dirty sheets, used condoms from the weekend, and tiny bottles bled dry to the last drop from the minibar.

With the gringo on his back, even though it was only five in the morning, Héctor couldn't walk down Reforma without sooner or later having to explain himself, so he climbed into a taxi and dashed off to look for an all-night drugstore. The driver, completely understanding, lent more to the attempt at an explanation than the detective did.

"No doubt, it was the cops who screwed him, right, kid? They're pigs, all of them!"

When they got to the Gigante Pharmacy, open twenty-four hours a day, specializing in that nocturnal toothache, in that sudden gastritis, in the fall of the body's sugar level, in the providential bottle of aspirin to keep a piece of your head from falling off, the night manager refused to come within a foot and a half of the gringo and only after twenty pleas from the detective did he agree to sell him bandages, hydrogen peroxide, and adhesive tape. Dick was starting to turn purple. He had a cut four or five inches long above his left eye, a small gash on his neck, and his lips were torn. Héctor sat him down on the curb of the parking lot and revealed his healing skills, which he had picked up from a movie about Florence Nightingale, the nurse-angel of the Crimean War. He had watched it six or seven times.

When the gringo asked for a cigarette in his Spanish full of mangled r's, Héctor decided to take him for a walk in Chapultepec. The sun was rising, a few reddish clouds circled around in the sky. It was a strange morning color.

The boat rentals, patronized by truant high school students during the week, didn't open for nearly another hour, so the detective whiled away the time by walking his gringo around the outskirts of the zoo and the Museum of Modern Art. Finally, sitting in the boat, as the North American rowed, Héctor tried to cash in on the favor and posed a question:

"And how did you earn that prize on your face?" the detective said, sticking his hand in the water and contemplating the wake his fingers were making.

"Who are you?"

"No, the one who heals is the one who asks the questions," Héctor answered in his engineering-manual English, substantially better than Dick's Spanish.

"I'm a reporter," the gringo answered, switching to English and dropping the oars. He searched through the pocket on the top part of his New York Yankees jacket and took out some crumpled-up press credentials from *Rolling Stone* magazine.

Beyond the bruises and bandages, he had a sad face, a timid look, black hair, and a sharp nose. Héctor figured they were more or less the same age.

"What business do you have with Luke Estrella?"

"Who is Luke Estrella?"

"The Cuban who broke your face."

"Oh, Betancourt . . . I wanted to interview him."

"Yeah, that much one can see," Héctor said. One bold swan started following the wake Belascoarán's fingers were leaving in the water. Héctor quickly withdrew his hand. You never knew what kind of mutations the Mexico City climate could produce in swans.

"And who is this Betancourt? What does he do?"

"Who are you? What do you do?" the gringo answered.

"Hell, it's a very long story," Héctor said.

A boat with a bunch of teenagers pulled up to the spot where the reporter and the detective had stopped theirs. The swans approached. Héctor figured the students must have left a trail of stale bread or corn. The swans of the lake, so different from the ducks at home, seemed gloomy, carnivorous, sad.

"That always happens to me when I come to Mexico, all the stories are long, very long, and no one seems to have enough time to tell them."

"I suspect that not even gringo reporters have the patience anymore."

"If we keep fucking around about our stories, the current will take us to the Panama Canal," Dick said, showing his first smile of the morning through his split lip. "I need at least two beers to decide between exchanging my story for yours or telling you a pile of shit."

"I could have a couple of Cokes while I decide if I should put you back in the hall where I found you and figure something out while watching the Cuban smash your face in again."

"While I row, we could start by agreeing on what our Cuban's name is."

"Luke Estrella," Héctor said.

"Gary Betancourt," Dick said.

"It seems to me we'll end up knowing him by more names."

Dick started rowing in search of beer. The disappointed swans abandoned the boat's wake.

V

The Story of Luke Estrella/Gary Betancourt as Told
by Dick
(Just as Héctor Belascoarán Shayne would later
remember it)

You always find the people who will interest you later when you're looking for others. That's a kind of unwritten rule. The best stories will appear like tatters hanging off other stories that in the end will be eclipsed. I believe in accidents, and then I believe that instinct adds up the accidents and tells you there's something there. Lastly, I believe in the stubbornness that allows you to find it.

If that is rule number one, rule number two also applies. It says, as far as I recall, that the guy who interests you is the one who is not where he should be, the one who stands out in the photo: the black man on a South African tennis team, the shoeshiner having a champagne cocktail in the palace, the New Zealander general getting a pedicure in a brothel in Madrid, the Mexican minister digging ditches with a community work brigade in Managua, the Broadway actress standing in line at a little restaurant where they sell empanadas in Lima.

There's still a third rule. The interesting one is the one whose name is not mentioned, the one they tell you isn't important, the one your usual sources seem to ignore.

Gary Betancourt fit the three rules, one after another. He appeared casually as a second reference while I was investigating the assassination of Olof Palme. No big deal, a very secondary mention in a newsletter of the Swedish groups in solidarity with Central America, mentioning that the Cuban had attempted to infiltrate them. They used that name, Gary Betancourt. I didn't give a shit about the story, I was trying to establish connections between the assassins of Orlando Letelier and those of Palme, chasing a rumor that had come slowly trickling down from a West German magazine that placed Townley in the affair—reviewing the papers, this story popped up. I didn't pay him the slightest attention, but my secretary filed the paper. The name reappeared as the investigation advanced, again it seemed unimportant, one of the Cuban *gusanos* who collaborated with the DINA, the Chilean Secret Service's envoy in the assassination of Letelier, but nothing important, his name was mentioned in reference to the rental of a couple of cars and a go-between job. At that time, a friend of mine had published a mention of Betancourt, the talkative type who in a conversation had commented that he hadn't been mixed up in the Letelier story because he was playing in the major leagues with the CIA. With statements like that you could fill a volume as big as the *Encyclopaedia Britannica*. At any rate, he was the only nexus between the assassinations of Letelier and Palme. Or rather, he was the nonexistent nexus. It wasn't enough for even an item of three hundred fifty words. I reviewed the little

Swedish newsletter again. The precise words were that the guy had been roaming the country trying to get into the committees, and that by the time he was denounced, he had disappeared. The dates coincided with the murder of Palme. I followed other leads.

Two weeks later, I passed a little card with his name to the magazine's department of documentation and they returned it to me with a couple of stapled press clips. In '76, he had been the proprietor of a couple of pornographic magazine shops in Miami, the ones said to launder the Cuban mafia's dirty money. The other clip was in connection to an act of Brigade 2506 that said he had been one of the speakers at the Bay of Pigs anniversary event. I liked the character, but I had nothing, not even one reason to investigate him. That's why I asked a friend of mine who worked as a fortune-teller outside Disneyland about Gary Betancourt and she told me to go to hell. Her business was an imprecise science, not the *Washington Post* data bank.

In this business, the only truly trustworthy thing is the memory. So when, six months later, I sent an information request to the Department of Immigration about the number of Vietnamese living in Los Angeles County, I added an appendix requesting data on Gary Betancourt. They sent me a sheet full of bureaucratic verbiage stating that Lutgardo Betancourt Estrella had been naturalized as an American in '65, becoming Gary Betancourt. He offered a pharmacy in Miami as a reference. The interesting part is that they had sent me the wrong copy, one on which after the final references, the sending of the copy with the answer to an office of uninterpretable abbreviations in Fort Lauderdale had been jotted down.

Later, I discovered, of course, that the office, according to the highly reliable Bell Company, did not exist.

I've got a friend in a corner of the Reagan administration who occasionally whispers something my way, "things going around out there." When I mentioned Gary Betancourt to him, he said he'd never heard of him in his life, was he a new hire for the Baltimore Orioles to improve their outfield? But he smiled three seconds longer than he should have.

Then I started studying the matter in earnest.

I could start by looking for connections between Betancourt and the CIA or by trying to enter his territory. I caught a flight to Florida.

I've gone swimming in Miami three times and it is like sinking in a pool of water while others watch you drown. Nobody knows anything, the rules are different, the borders between law and order are flimsier than the ones in Dodge City in the middle of the last century. There is a marginal world that runs several cities superimposed on the visible city, cities more real than the ones in the tourism brochures the mayor hands out when he's running for reelection. I could have gone either alone or with the people from the *Miami Herald*, a paper that has grown in national importance based on throwing a few blind blows, often with noteworthy results. If I shared what I had on Betancourt with them, one of two things would have happened: they would have thought the whole thing was crap and that it wasn't worth getting involved in, or they would have thought there was something there and they would've started swimming at my side like sharks; later they would have thrown me the bones left over from the cadaver of the story. It was quite evident that I had to walk alone.

I started with the obvious. Betancourt wasn't listed in the phone book. The pharmacy where he worked in 1965 didn't exist; it was possible it never existed. In the Association of Ex-Soldiers of the Bay of Pigs he was not registered; someone remembered that yes, he had spoken at a meeting, but he was not a member of the brigade. In the Cuban exiles' files, only the known facts appeared. A secretary smiled at me and made the sign of someone who sniffs cocaine when I mentioned Betancourt to her. When I asked about him explicitly, she said she didn't know him. If anything turns me on, it's ghosts. I was going up a level. The FBI in Florida: Betancourt? Unofficially, they had a few things pending with him, but he didn't belong to them, he hadn't been around Miami for two years. What things? Drug trafficking, no big deal, maybe the DEA would give me some of his booty. A car stolen on a drunken binge, does anybody care? No, no one, we all have a couple of kids (in my case it's my father and an uncle), who've done that once. The arms trafficking thing bothered them. What traffic? What arms? For whom? Arms? We didn't say that, or did we?

As I discovered, the Cuban ghost and I had a mutual friend, an art gallery owner. He knew Betancourt slightly. He occasionally accompanied a general friend of his to buy paintings. A general from where? From those countries down below. Colombian, Bolivian, Salvadoran? Mexican. Mexican? Or Peruvian, from those countries. Were the paintings worth much? No, nothing, nah.

A woman who lived with him. Nothing. Nothing? He owned a few porn stores. They weren't around anymore, one was now an ice cream store. The American dream, all porn stores can be transformed into ice cream stores. He hadn't seen him around the city for a couple of months. Months, not years? Months. If only it were years; he wasn't worth the dirt he walked on.

I bumped into a friend of a friend of mine who, according to my original friend, knew everything, but it would cost to make him talk. He was a very young Chinese guy. What had he lost in Miami? Him or Betancourt? Both. Betancourt. The rest was business. Betancourt was with the CIA. Everybody knew it. He was one of the recruits of '62. Didn't he come to the States in '65? No, '62, when they created the base, the J.M. Wave. Later, it hit the same luck most of the bases did, when they were busted because in '62 the Cuban government had filled the Agency with moles. Some paid for others, Cuba ended up costing them dearly. They were dismantled, even though he kept talking. There are no borders. You start an arms deal for the CIA and finish it for a group of Puerto Rican gangsters in New Jersey. You sell a little shit to the DEA guys, then you resell it to the Colombians, and you end up building a company to sell illegal crocodile leather because the business popped up along the way and you end up laundering the money of some people, informing others, and conducting commerce with the remaining easily duped mortals. Who are you? Who do you work for? There comes a time when only you know. Not even those who pay you are sure anymore. The business dealings of the Company are obscure, like the designs of Confucius. Was I from the CIA? Are you from the CIA? Are we both from the CIA? Shit, if so our ops should have already reached an agreement at Langley and we wouldn't be wasting our time. Speaking of time, that's fifty dollars.

I went back to Los Angeles with the conviction that I'd been running around futilely. I continued the investigation over the phone for a week without getting anything. Suddenly, an assistant to one of the members of the Senate Agency Oversight Subcommittee called me, we arranged to meet, he was in California looking for the woman of his dreams. Did he find her? No, deep down, he was gay. So? He told me I was wasting time, that Betancourt was a little rat and that he hadn't been active for years. If I wanted an interesting story, why didn't I delve into the world of retirees? There were a lot of loose rats. They had recruited them, they had used them in covert operations, in dirty work all over the planet, and now they didn't know what to do with them, they made the worst office workers. Not even close to the traditional loyalty of the natives, not even close to Gunga Din or the Apache scouts that Charlton Heston used. A couple of hours after we left each other, he called me at the magazine, requested maximum confidentiality, and suggested I tell Betancourt to go to hell and start investigating Sid Valdés-Vasco, that that guy was pure Texas hamburger meat. I didn't understand the metaphor. I didn't pay him any attention. I didn't have any money. I started working on a report on the water problems between northern and southern California, then another about drugs in Los Angeles high schools, then, with an investigative team, on the Catholic Church's business dealings in Texas and New Mexico. Finally, on the way home, in a lousy mood on a day when my cigarettes tasted just plain bad, it occurred to me to send a little paper to Documentation with the name Sid Valdés-Vasco. They sent back a photo of Betancourt. Divine, all roads lead to Rome. Even the ones going to Rome. Papers started coming to my hands. A mention in the book by Robbins on Air America, the CIA's airline. Valdés-Vasco, Vevé, had organized the arms shipments to guys who worked for Savimbi, the pro–South African guerrilla from Angola, and his organization, UNITA. More papers, a mention of his intervention in the relations between the DEA and the CIA in the matter of the war between the true Mafia and the Colombian mafia and, therefore, all the political connections of the affair. He was the man who had negotiated in the name of the CIA with the Bolivian coke-dollar generals, to break with Colombia.

My friend from the Senate called me again a week ago and said: "Mexico City, Hotel Presidente Chapultepec, December seventh."

And so it was. I arrived, I knocked on the door, I asked him for an interview. I was interested in the Gunga Din story, Apache scouts, those who'd run dirty operations, the Cold War artisans who'd gone into early retirement. He smiled and hit me right in the eye. I didn't even have a chance to take out my tape recorder.

VI

I have lived long enough to not be sure of anything.

Nicholas Guild

Estrella–Betancourt–Valdés-Vasco, of course, had disappeared. Héctor wasn't even pissed off; in fact, he'd expected it. In the afternoon, the Cuban had packed his bags and checked out of the Presidente Chapultepec. These things happened to stupid detectives. And Héctor deserved it.

And now how the hell was he going to find him again? In a place like Mexico City, with its twenty million desperate survivors, we are all a needle in a haystack. Estrella-Betancourt still hadn't kicked up any dust, he'd left no traces of any kind of relationships, he'd revealed no contacts, hadn't fallen in love with anyone, had shown no predilection for beef tacos or a certain park bench. So it was impossible to look for him. He had simply vanished in a city that takes pleasure in anonymity. Héctor knew it would be a waste of time to try to trace his steps by the taxis in front of the hotel, or the bellhop.

There was one revolting option that Héctor pondered in silence under the casual vigilance of the gringo reporter, who seemed to possess a remarkable ability to take things calmly when he was drinking beer. A goddamn awful possibility because it basically consisted of inverting the game. When you can't find someone in Mexico City, you can scream that he is a son of a goddamned bitch over the local sound system of Azteca Stadium and repeat it over the amplifiers at a Tri rock concert and then broadcast it on spots on Radio One Thousand, and then he will probably start looking for you. And that didn't strike Héctor as terribly funny. Inverting the roles, knowing that the other will play the game only in the remote case that it interests him, and therefore with an advantage. Becoming the waiting one, the target silhouette again . . . He had had too many dark experiences in the recent past to be able to commit to that without a couple of metaphorical scorpions crawling across his back. He decided to give Dick a piece of his mind. They were eating hamburgers in the Sanborn's on Aguascalientes as they contemplated the fifteen-year-old idiots of golden youth.

"And why exactly do you want Estrella-Betancourt? Are you serious about writing a story on CIA retirees?"

"Because I'm sure that there's a conflict between a faction of the senatorial committee and the CIA, and that's why they pushed me onto Betancourt, to shed some light on it. None of the deserter business, there's an operation running in Mexico, and it must be dirty enough for these guys to be interested in my lifting the shroud a little. Why do you want him?"

"I suspect the guy deserves to go sit his ass on a concrete bench in a Mexican jail; I like Alicia's theory."

"I've got a little money from the magazine for this kind of thing. Can I hire you to find him?"

"I've got a little cash from an inheritance, can I hire you to write an article, making you the target for him to find?" Héctor answered.

The detective and the reporter exchanged smiles.

"What the hell could he be doing in Mexico?"

"Almost anything."

"In your little papers, your clips, your reports from friends of friends, was there any Mexican connection, some name that would link him to Mexico?" Héctor asked.

"Nothing," Dick responded, distracted as he contemplated the recently crossed legs of a woman two tables down. Héctor followed his gaze.

"What are you planning to do, then?" Héctor asked, discarding the possibility of playing bait.

"Nothing," Dick said, getting up to approach the pair of legs smiling at him. "I guess I'll take a vacation in Mexico, a week or two. An alcoholic vacation. I just got divorced and I was in Alcoholics Anonymous because my ex-wife wanted me to. Now I can have the luxury of being a public drunk again. And you?"

"I'll take a vacation, too. A teetotaler vacation," Héctor replied.

When he opened his eyes, he discovered he was surrounded by absolute darkness, different from the darkness of night locked in his room. There was no reflection of the street lamps, no noise of cars. When he moved his arm, he bumped into a wall. Sizing things up with his toes, he quickly met new borders. It was a tiny room. He felt for his gun in the holster under his arm, but all he was wearing were pajama tops. Being disarmed worried him. He pushed his hand gently in the only direction left to explore. The door opened. A few feet away, the window let in the neon light off the street. He had been sleeping in the closet.

"Absolute shit," he said to himself. He was completely twisted, his thighs were prickling from the rug chafing his naked skin. One of the ducks appeared at the door and Héctor almost killed it with one involuntary stamp of the foot. He tripped over his own shoes and, howling because he had stubbed the little toe of his left foot, went to lie down on the bed.

That was the only thing missing, he said to himself as he tried to control the pain with psychoprophylactic birthing methods. Tense-relax-tense. At what point had he decided to sleep in the closet? Who was the other self who was disorganizing his life? The pain in his toe was beginning to subside. Christ, at least it's not fractured, Héctor thought, regaining a positive attitude.

"And besides, it's not a bad night's sleep in that stupid closet. I have to put a pillow in there," he said out loud, now brimming with neopositivism.

He walked to the kitchen, opened a can of Alaskan crab and started eating it in spoonfuls. The clock in the kitchen showed 4:30. Halfway through the food, he stretched and went to the bathroom to get a towel and dry off his ass. As positive as the detective might be, there was still a sticky, icy sweat that ran down his spine. The sweat of a variety of mingled fears.

The ducks parked outside the bathroom door, making little sounds. Héctor followed them to the plate in the middle of the hall rug. They had tipped it over and it was full of droppings. He partially cleaned up the mess using the magazine *Plural*, an issue dedicated to the poetry of Outer Mongolia, then he filled the plate with water and gave them a cup of bread crumbs. He assumed correctly that the ducks were not interested in the Alaskan crab; still, he let them smell it and snub it. They were a couple of pretty stupid ducks, but not as stupid as one paranoid detective he knew who fell asleep in his bed and woke up in a closet.

He watched dawn break from the roof of the building while contemplating the doves eating stale tortillas, and the sun that appeared between the Scop Tower and the Mexican Aviation Tower. People who aren't what they were before always go around saying that sunrises aren't what they used to be. Héctor abstained from such a banality, and limited himself to thinking that something had broken between him and the city, that in some incomprehensible way the city was slipping through his hands before his eyes. "You can't die without losing things," he said to himself.

When he went down the stairs on the way to his office, he found Alicia sitting in front of the door to his building.

"I thought you didn't want to let me in," she told him, in the volatile accent of a Mexican who's been exchanging words six thousand feet above the ocean, who's lost phrases and found other new ones in airports and duty-free shops.

"I lost him," Héctor said, opening the door and motioning to invite her in.

"You've found him again," the woman said with a

smile. "He's leaving for Acapulco at nine thirty on the Mexicana flight."

"Can you feed the ducks?" Héctor asked as he jumped down the steps, and threw her the keys.

Héctor couldn't help it. He loved the bay. He looked and looked and it was still the best beach in the world. He even liked the hotel towers that hemmed in the sand and pushed it against the sea. La Roqueta, an island that seemed to have been placed there for the benefit of tourist excursions; the little sailboats; the colorful parachutes; the yachts; the nonexistent gringas (it seemed they were all Canadians now); even the surges of walking salespeople. The burning sun, the jungle around the corner on the highway going up, the sea so blue it seemed like a lie, the postcard afternoons (photographic fiction imitating reality) on Pie de la Cuesta, the waves to combat them on Condesa Beach, the grilled jumbo shrimp, the sound of the mariachis in the lobby of a hotel.

He didn't give a shit if Acapulco had been condemned by practically everyone. It was no longer the weekend paradise of Mexico City's middle class, now strangled by inflation. The ecologists were dissing the beaches and the ocean, which they denounced as being so polluted that even a petroleum worker would be repulsed to swim in it. The golden youth had emigrated to the Mexican Caribbean, leaving Acapulco in its antiquated, passé corner. The international tourists had gone to Puerto Vallarta and Manzanillo to pursue the

fantasy of "the night of the iguana." Even Acapulcans
said it wasn't what it used to be; only in Carlos Fuentes's
novels, with his ravings of the 1950s transported to the
present, did the bay seem alive. Carlos Fuentes was
one of the few serious guys left in the country, maybe
because he lived outside it.

In the mountains the destitute people clustered together and contemplated the beaches, which, even as
a shadow of what they were, continued to reveal the
world of the inaccessible others; but Héctor, always in
solidarity with border cities, with final cities, with the
ruins of others that reminded him of his own, remained
in love with Acapulco. He was thinking: in a few years
it will be an archaeological model and the masses will
come down from the mountains to take it over, and
then I will like it even more; when a legion of five-
year-old mulattoes holding the hands of their teachers,
dressed in old-fashioned, blue one-piece bathing suits,
go into the sea on the beach of the twin towers or the
Ritz. When the Hotel Pierre is a museum of old people
and fewer old pirates.

He thought all this from a beach at a distance, as he
let the sun scorch him and warm his scars. Through
the binoculars he studied alternately a big-bottomed
French woman in a tiny blue bikini and Luke Estrella.

Acapulco was driving him crazy and he'd only been
beachgoing for two days. He had given in to gluteal
contemplation. The asses fascinated him. In these
strange moments when he was lamenting being one-
eyed (because, say what you will, with one eye you see
less than with two), Héctor Belascoarán, sunbathing
detective, had compiled a catalogue of asses, democrat-

ically, without putting some before others, relishing them without debate. The sharp high asses of the skinny blondes; the rounded ones of the Japanese in black bikinis playing around a few feet from his hammock; the monumental ass of the Jamaican mulatto that bubbled over the material of the bikini, trying to escape on both sides; the heart-shaped asses of the University of Nuevo León professors celebrating their divorces; the low but wide ass of the cross-eyed Australian incessantly eating oysters. Resplendent asses, full of sun, oscillating to varying rhythms, rising and falling, moving in alternating buttocks, rising with a single bump of the hip, winking at the impartial observer. He was contemplating them like an expert in a museum of modern art; Héctor assumed the attitude of a privileged spectator.

All this was possible because Estrella wasn't giving him too much trouble. Alone, solitary, silent, sunbathing, getting wet when he had to to cool off the skin, eating a lot, taking long siestas on the terrace off his room, which Héctor observed through his binoculars every once in a while from inside his room. Calm, waiting for something. Smiling condescendingly at the looks that a few single women directed his way from time to time. Marvelous, Estrella. He wasn't being a drag, and Héctor, instead of despairing because the investigation wasn't going anywhere, had devoted himself to the rapture of buttocks. He had seen thousands in those two days. And perhaps the time had come to initiate a world competition, assigning points to their proprietors: so many points for the shape, so many for

visual impact, so many for the erotic message, so many
for the insinuation some of the bathing suits offered,
so many for the vulgarity of the movement. He could
do it in categories: flyweight, bantamweight, and heavy-
weight. Or he could establish an all-around . . .

Héctor swallowed a swig of his Coca-Cola with lime
and then pointed the binoculars toward Estrella. He
was facing the ocean, sitting in a folding chair, his
eyes closed, his face getting direct sun, his eyes hidden
behind the inevitable dark glasses. Héctor turned forty-
five degrees and contemplated the ass of a woman
selling contraband Colombian clothes who was passing
through Acapulco on one of her business trips between
Houston and Barranquilla. She was wearing a gold suit
and her entire right cheek had escaped from the brief
bikini bottom, a round cheek, lamentably paler than
her thighs, lamentably with a small rash, probably the
result of sweat. He deducted two points, although the
movement was frankly good.

With a little luck, Estrella had come to Acapulco to
simply sit in the sun.

"Room 604 received two calls yesterday. The first
time he wasn't in his room and they left him a message
that he was invited to a dinner party tonight," the Hotel
Maris receptionist told him. Héctor put a twenty-
thousand-peso bill on the counter.

"Do you have change?"

The receptionist went to the cash register and returned with a couple of one-thousand-peso bills and a little piece of paper folded with them. Héctor thanked her with a smile.

The detective walked toward his hotel, which was on the same beach only five hundred feet away. On the way he studied the paper. It had six figures: 11-57-04. A few minutes later, in the solitude of his room, he dialed the number.

"Attorney Garduño's residence," answered a woman's voice.

Héctor hung up. With the aid of the phone book, he discarded five Garduños and matched the sixth with the phone number. An address near the Convention Center was the booty.

He was in the shower, getting ready for a dinner to which he had not been invited, when he heard knuckles knocking on the door.

Héctor looked in his suitcase for his gun. He hadn't been able to carry it those last few days, it didn't fit in his bathing suit. He loaded the cartridge and approached the door with a slight tremble in his legs. He chewed on his mustache.

"Hello, it's me, Dick," said the reporter's face, less black-and-blue than it had been a couple of days ago.

"Come in, old man," Héctor answered, flinging the gun onto the bed.

"Did you find him?"

Héctor nodded. He felt an obligation to inform the reporter that Estrella wasn't really that important, that what was going on in Acapulco in terms of asses was major-league, but he restrained himself and simply said, "Tonight we're going to a dinner party, pal."

*   *   *

It was a party of five, but the five were deeply surrounded by assistants, lackeys, secretaries, bodyguards. It was a masculine and well-armed society, to judge by the bulges under the arms of the aides. Through the binoculars, Héctor tried to identify each of the participants in the dinner, to distinguish them. There was the old man with very short white hair, a crew cut over a dark, pockmarked face. There was the young North American (Anglo, no doubt), in a white sport jacket with wide lapels designed by a phantom cousin of Christian Dior; there was the young guy with the pointed nose, swarthy, in dark glasses, who almost never spoke, whom the bodyguards treated with respect; there was the middle-aged man, silent now, who had argued bitterly with Estrella shortly after the introductions were made and who was indubitably Garduño, the owner of the house, because he had received the guests, ordered the servants to bring drinks, and moved around the house like the only possible proprietor.

"Let me guess," Dick said, snatching the binoculars from Belascoarán. They were leaning against a car, under partial cover from the trees, on a small hill behind the house at the end of a dead-end road in the still not fully constructed resort. "The old man with white hair traffics in ancient Mexican coins."

"You're wrong, old friend. He's a military man or a navy officer, probably retired. And yes, he is Mexican. What do you say about the gringo?"

"His name is Jerome and he is the CIA's chief of operations in Central America. He usually lives in San José, Costa Rica."

Héctor looked at his friend with more respect than usual.

"The long-nosed young guy in dark glasses?"

"Is he Nicaraguan? His face looks familiar," Dick said.

"If he's Nicaraguan, he's been living in Mexico for a while. Look at the way he loves the hot sauce, he smokes Mexican cigarettes, he's got those good manners of the 1950s middle class, he's wearing a Roberts suit. But you might be right, those are the contras of the middle class."

"Can you see the label from here?"

"No, man, I'm guessing."

Héctor took back the binoculars and focused his gaze on Estrella. After the initial clash with the owner of the house he'd kept quiet, watching and half smiling, as if this weren't about him, eating abundantly and drinking all the wine poured into his glass. In that instant Dick left the detective, walked among the weeds toward the car, and came back with a Minolta endowed with an enormous telephoto lens. He started snapping the men dining on the terrace a hundred yards away. The smell of the sea was swept in by a gentle breeze.

"I'm turning into a man without passion. A few years ago, curiosity would have forced me to creep in through the garden until I got under the terrace, to see if I could fish out some scrap of conversation," Belascoarán said in Spanish.

"What the hell are they talking about?" Dick asked, not having understood the detective's spiel.

"The weather, the natural beauty of Acapulco. It's a group of amiable investors who want to launch a new travel agency. Are you sure the gringo is CIA?"

"We've met," Dick said, not going into the story.

"The skinny guy they all treat with so much coddling, the one with the pointy nose. I don't like the way he smiles one bit," Héctor said.

"Me neither."

"He arrived in a blue car, a Ford. With three gunmen. We could wait for him beyond the bend, on the side of the Diana statue."

"Shouldn't we wait to see how this ends?"

"Dessert was over a while ago."

The woman was dancing naked on the table. Every once in a while, her sex shook six inches away from the pointed nose of the man they had followed. The music was a tropical beat but the woman had lost it a good while ago and danced following who knows what internal sounds, possibly from indigestion. The cabaret was a democratic hovel in the center of the city, where two friendly cops searched the clients at the door (to disarm them) and the greatest spectacle was a couple of dogs screwing in the entrance. At least that seemed to interest the customers more than what was happening on the table. The cops in blue had given a military salute to the man with the pointy nose, who was now counting bills, the woman's sex swinging close to his face not seeming to distract him. The bills did not come floating through the air to the table. Every so often, some timid gorilla approached the man, handed him a wad, as if apologizing for the affront, not daring to sit down with him.

"Who is it?" Dick asked.

"From his manners, he has to be the chief of the Judicial Police," Héctor answered, feeling a long shiver run up his spine.

"What shit are we getting mixed up in?" the gringo reporter asked, throwing back a swig of his double tequila.

"I have no idea, but my good eye is starting to blink."

"Do you feel sick?"

"No, I'm fine, I think it's just fear," the detective said, finishing his Pepsi in one long gulp.

A sweaty fat man approached their table, put his hands between the empty glasses, and offered them a photo album.

"You can choose, boss. They're the best around. House calls, too. They come to your room with a bottle. Clean, they bring your condom, two condoms in case you're a multiple screwer. They do everything. Everything, boss!"

Héctor flipped through the pages of the photo album curiously. It could easily have been a family album with pictures of weddings and sweet sixteen parties, bachelor parties, and Grandma's golden wedding anniversary. But they were sad photos of naked teenagers with looks and poses that hoped to evoke eroticism and rather seemed more like material for a book by Lévi-Strauss.

"I've got machines, dogs, hags, boys, pregnant

women. Everything, I've got everything, all you have
to do is ask, boss."

Héctor passed the album to the gringo reporter,
wanting nothing to do with the affair. The man with
the pointy nose finished counting, looked around the
joint, made a gesture and the music vanished. A busboy
put a bottle of tequila in the hands of one of the assistants, who in turn brought it to the boss's table. From
a back room, through a curtain, came three guitarists,
playing the tune of a bolero.

The woman who was dancing naked came down off
the table. The music of the guitars seemed to have
muted all the other noises in the room. The fat man
grabbed his album without insisting. Then the man
with the pointy nose stood up, stuck the rolls of bills
in his pants pockets, and motioned to the guitar players.
They segued into "Nosotros," and he started singing
along. He was out of tune.

You don't ask too many questions in a city where
you don't have friends. You mull over each thing, you
add up little facts, you don't get big stories. Two days
later, as he drank an iced coffee on the terrace of his
hotel and contemplated the light in Estrella's room and
the sky of the Acapulco bay, full of dancing stars, the
detective told the North American reporter the five
names he had found in two days of snooping around.
Two days, in fact, in which the gringo had disappeared
on him. There wasn't much, not much at all. The five
guys who had been dining that evening:

Estrella-Betancourt. Attorney Roberto Garduño, lawyer for transnational hotel companies; divorced two months earlier from a girl of golden youth, the daughter of the owner of a watch factory; jai alai player, local champion; owner of two discos. The skinny, long-nosed man was named Julio Reyes and he was not the commander, just the group chief of Acapulco's Judicial Police; a fan of romantic music; winner of two or three radio contests; he was not from Guerrero, he was born in the south, in Chiapas, near the border; there was talk that he had once cut off a man's head with a machete; prostitutes loved him, he didn't give them a hard time, he didn't touch them, once he'd been in love with one of them who fled for the border, they said he dedicated his best songs to her. A gringo from the CIA called Jerome. A retired admiral, Julio Pacheco, who was now the proprietor of a coconut farm for the manufacture of oil on the Costa Grande of Guerrero.

"I was always afraid of riding a bike," Dick said, sipping his coffee. "I went straight from crawling to cars. Very North American, that. Still, I would trade all the Pontiacs, Fords, and Chevrolets I have ever driven for a good bike ride. You long for what you've never had."

Héctor studied the reporter. When had he gotten drunk and with what?

"I have a son I haven't seen in a year and I've always wanted to buy him a bike, but his mother won't let me. I think I owe my obsession with bicycles to that. See, I'm a father without a son. Psychiatrists don't understand shit about all that. Mine tries to persuade me to lose weight instead of persuading me to just buy a bike once and for all."

Héctor walked to the bathroom, reconstructing the reporter's movements, and found two empty gin bottles in the sink. Motherfucker, another lunatic. In the middle of a conversation, he went into the bathroom and drank gin straight from the bottle.

"And now they make them with the handlebars in the shape of horns, but before ..." He swung around to see Héctor carrying the cadaver of the gin. "You drink the same brand?"

Héctor shook his head.

"Do you know that joke about the guy who picked up a girl in the woods and she sat on the handlebars of the bike and when they got into town she thanked him for the ride on the handlebars of the bike and he said to her, 'No, this bike doesn't have handlebars'?"

Dick didn't wait for the detective to smile; he turned around, stumbling into the base of one of the beds, and rummaged through his carpetbag. He took out a new bottle, sparkling ... The light in Estrella's room went off. Héctor walked to the door.

"I'll be back in a minute."

The hotel orchestra playing by the pool was engrossed in a nameless bossa nova. He walked along the beach, barely lit by the moon, toward the neighboring hotel. He went up the stairs leading to the pool, they were grilling lobster under a gazebo. A new orchestra was playing another bossa nova. Héctor pricked up his ears, trying to hear the one they were playing back at his hotel; suddenly it seemed very important to know whether it was the same one. He couldn't tell. Estrella was sitting by the side of the pool, dangling his toes in the water, frolicking. Héctor stayed close to where he could smell the lobsters cooking in their own juice. Estrella was a theatrical guy, with his white linen suits and his sky blue shirts, his dark glasses even on moonless nights, his curly hair with a few silver strands, his rhythmical gestures that made him seem like a retired rumba dancer.

The whole thing was amusing. If he wanted to follow Alicia's suggestions, all he had to do was reintroduce Estrella to his friend Julio Reyes, the group chief of the Judicial Police in Acapulco, and tell him that the Cuban had stuck his nose in some foul play. No, it wasn't funny at all. In this country, all that remained was Apache justice. First he would have to know, then he would have to find the roads on which God's justice would reach Luke Estrella and punish him for going around torturing a woman who liked Armando Manzanero's boleros and all that, while evading another guy who sang José Feliciano boleros in brothels.

A waiter approached the chair where Estrella was reclining and took his order. Shortly thereafter, he returned with two cocktails. Héctor walked, bordering the pool on the opposite side looking for a new place of observation; he found it on a few deck chairs near where they stored the towels. He reclined on one of them, still in the darkness. Estrella was toying with his cocktail now. A woman in a radiantly white evening gown passed beside him, it had an extraordinarily low back, closing the dress almost at the birth of her buttocks. She shot a look at Héctor, sitting in the darkness in his dark blue bathing suit and his black T-shirt, his left eye covered by the patch. The look was prolonged for an instant in a friendly, languid, complicitous smile. The woman circled the edge of the pool. When she approached Estrella, he stood up with the two cocktails in his hands. The woman stopped and started conversing with him. They knew each other. Héctor waited for the Cuban to besiege her with flattery. Nothing like that came to pass. Estrella didn't even shoot a glance at the naked back when the woman looked for a chair to sit down next to him; he limited himself to pulling out a small book from one of the pockets of his white suit and took a few notes about what the woman was telling him. Héctor felt a sharp pang of fear. Why had the blonde with the low back smiled at him?

VII

We now know that locking yourself in serves for nothing, any disaster takes death to the safest refuge.

José Emilio Pacheco

When he woke up he was lying on the rug and the gringo reporter was staring at him; a bottle of gin (a new one?) affectionately rocking in his arms.

"You have nightmares," Dick informed him.

"I suppose I do, I never remember them," Héctor said, standing up and walking with difficulty to the bathroom.

"What's your favorite song?"

" 'La Bamba,' the new version by Los Lobos, it's much better than the original version by Trini Lopez; although the truth is, I feel affection for that one . . ."

The detective stuck his face under the gush of water in the sink, not daring to look at it first. The water was cold. What the hell was he doing in Acapulco with a drunk gringo reporter for a roommate and pursuing a Cuban *gusano* who was a CIA agent? There were ten other equally exciting and idiotic possibilities. Start a bakery in the middle of Puebla, work as a peon in the new archaeological excavations of Teotihuacán, become a groupie of the Symphonic Orchestra of the State of Mexico and follow them to all their concerts.

How wonderful! One day in Ocampo, another in Lerma, finally Toluca.

Dick started talking, staring into space.

"The heat drives me crazy. Not suddenly, slowly. I swear that when I got to Acapulco I had the most serious intention of lending you a hand with this story," he said, moving his head from one side to another, as if saying no. "But I don't know, it's something superior to my strength. Strange stories start coming into my head. I remember a cousin of mine who takes care of dolphins at Sea World and I get jealous . . ."

"What are we doing here?" Héctor asked.

"Following my Gary Betancourt, the famous Sid Valdés-Vasco, in other words, your Luke Estrella," the gringo said to the detective, flopping onto the bed and taking a good swig of gin. Neither his bed or Héctor's was unmade; the detective had slept on the rug, the reporter had either spent the night standing up on the terrace or had gone out there before Héctor got back.

"That's what I thought," the detective said, putting on a Coca-Cola T-shirt.

"You wear imperialist T-shirts?" Dick asked.

"It's Coca-Cola Mexico, made by honest Mexican workers in bottling factories in cities as healthy, Mexican, and productive as Iguala or Jalapa, or in rancid suburbs like Tlanepantla," Héctor responded, thinking that insanity might be contagious.

"That bastard with the dolphins, he knows what life is," Dick said before falling asleep, the bottle of gin miraculously safe in his clutch.

Héctor approached him and took it away, then went out on the balcony. Estrella was on his hotel terrace.

Héctor went back into the room and got his binoculars. Was he looking toward his room? Impossible. He was over a hundred yards away. Damned Cuban, son of a fucking bitch, with those dark glasses you could never know what he was watching.

Maybe Dick was right, the dolphin guy lived a life straight out of the movies.

Héctor drew his nose to the bottle of gin, he smelled it cautiously. The aroma was sickly sweet. Maybe he could throw it down the toilet, then refill it with water and sugar and Dick wouldn't notice. He remembered something his friend René Cabrera said. They were sentences that suddenly came to his memory. René was the best poet of his generation, but he had insisted on being a scientist, and was running around out there in the state of Veracruz doing anthropology. He left the room with the sentence dancing in his head: "How lucky are dwarfs, who see the world so beautifully and from below."

Thumbing through brochures that offered love boat excursions, he waited patiently in the lobby of the neighboring hotel for Estrella to appear on the way to the dining room; when the Cuban did so, he took the elevator to the sixth floor. He sought out the woman who went around making up the rooms and approached her with a smile.

"I left my key downstairs, señorita, could you just open the door to 604 for me?"

The woman didn't even look at him. Héctor blessed

the rare honesty that still existed, and entered Estrella's room without looking back. The notebook he was looking for was on the little night table. Before leafing through it, he noted the plane ticket in the open drawer of the bureau and the .45 sticking out of the half-open suitcase. The guy had five identical white suits, he discovered upon examining the closet. He must not believe in the virtues of Mexican laundry. The notebook was a small calendar, totally blank with the exception of one page toward the back on which three figures were written. He memorized them.

In his hotel room, Dick was asleep. Héctor shook him a little and read the three figures to him.

"What is this?"

"The wholesale prices of a quarter ounce of cocaine in New York, Los Angeles, and Miami one week ago."

"Are you serious? Don't tease."

"That's what I think, let's see, say them again. They could also be the price of the rates for one line of advertising in the *New York Times*, *Miami Herald*, and *Los Angeles Times*."

"Six hundred thirty-one, four hundred thirteen, five hundred eighteen."

"Shit, I was right. I'm more alert asleep," Dick said and he reimmersed himself in the nightmare the detective had interrupted. Héctor looked at him with absolute distrust.

Estrella met with two of the table companions of that night again in one of Garduño's discos. A spot on the Costera, lit up by quartz reflectors that cast a "here I am" to the sky, and with music that deafened for a thousand feet around. Observing the variety of cars pulling up and parked in the back, it was clear that the place called Cleopatra was quite fashionable. Jerome, Estrella, and Garduño met at a table full of champagne bottles facing the dance floor and they were the only three serious members of the panel of judges for Miss Bikini Acapulco '88. Héctor thought that if there were something to be understood here, no one had shown him the synopsis. What the hell were three guys suspected of hatching dirty business on an international scale doing acting as the jury for a beauty contest?

As the night progressed he consumed Coca-Colas at the bar like a desperate man, and Héctor hated them a little more. They were voting for the wrong one. In the first round, they disqualified his favorite, a girl from the Gulf with long, dark legs; in the second vote, they left the tiny blonde with elevated breasts in fifth place. They were a trio of bastards with bad taste who liked skinny *Vogue* cover girls.

For a while, the detective put the contest aside and studied them attentively. They seemed like the best friends in the world, they elbowed one another, whispered things in one another's ears, poured one another's drinks. These guys really loved each other, they acted like they'd just come from a high school prom where they had been the three most mafioso pals, the three inseparable monsters. When the winner lifted the bouquet of red roses and let Garduño put a banner on her saying "Señorita Bikini Acapulco '88," Héctor thought that this little girl would never know in whose hands the decision that created her triumph had been. Had she known, instead of going around showing off her breasts, she might have devoted herself to selling lottery tickets.

The detective decided to abandon the disco because he sensed that from the stage, as he embraced the winner, Garduño was watching him. Outside, the heat was sticky, it reeked, the trash was being picked up.

Dick wasn't in the hotel room. There was a new empty bottle of gin in the toilet bowl. Héctor removed it so he could pee. Then he fell on the bed and opened a Philip José Farmer science fiction novel he had bought in the hotel lobby. At some point while reading he fell asleep.

The next day he woke up under the bed, two guns in his hands, his fingers wrapped like hooks around the triggers. Fortunately, he'd left the safeties on; otherwise he would have polished off every cockroach and mosquito in the room before being able to repent. He had to put both arms under a gush of water for some time, alternating hot and cold before he got his blood to circulate normally again.

He needed allies. He couldn't keep exposing himself on Acapulco nights with his giveaway eye, they would end up poking out the good eye he had left and giving it to the sharks or the dolphins, which in this case were the same, no matter how well Dick's cousin trained them. He pulled out the phone.

Macario Rendueles, the saxophonist, had been born in Acapulco. He started dialing long-distance to Mexico City. When he got his friend on the other end of the line, he discovered that he didn't really know what to ask him. There were all kinds of noises on the phone. "Belas, how the hell did you get lost in the pearl of the Pacific? Son of a bitch, the line is so bad. In this stupid city, at this point the rats talk on the phone while they eat the cables."

"Do you know a countryman of yours named Roberto Garduño? A lawyer. You know anyone I can trust who can tell me how the underworld works around here?"

"It's pure underworld there, pal, why do you think I grabbed my saxophone and split to roam different pastures? That city is cursed, man; can't you see it's pure set, pure papier-mâché, pure appearance for tourists. When the last plane takes off, they take down the decorations and the stupid beaches are left empty . . . ." Macario said and he started playing the saxophone over the speakerphone. "What should I play for you, stupid Belas?"

"A free version of '*Blue Moon.*' "

"You earned an answer, my good man. Talk to Raúl Murguía, he told me something about that Garduño; the truth is I can't remember very well now. He's living in Tabasco, you'll find him at the Museo de La Venta. Do you remember Raúl Murguía?" Macario Rendueles said, and he let loose with a new piece. Héctor gave him a shot for the first thirty seconds then hung up.

With the tune of "Love for Sale" dancing in his head, Héctor recalled Raúl Murguía. They had worked together a couple of years back. He was an anthropologist who had been affiliated with southeastern museums and, to halt the smuggling of small objets d'art, pyramid fragments, indigenous little idols, he had created a brigade of Mayans on motorcycles with shotguns: the Jacinto Canek Motorized Brigade. The thievery dropped, but they chased him out of his job because he scared the tourists. Half an hour later, he had him on the phone. The answer surprised him.

"Garduño? The one from Acapulco? Of course I know who he is. That guy is no more and no less than the fence of the most important stolen archaeological objects in this stupid country. That bastard knows every basement in Houston and Dallas where they have pieces from Mexican museums. Did you know that it's in among millionaires in Texas to have some piece stolen from a Mexican museum? It has real cachet. One day, in the middle of a barbecue, you ask your buddies (also millionaires) if they want to see something. You lead them down halls and steel-plated doors, all half mysterious. You have to have an adequate basement for the secret museum and there, in a black velvet recess, is a Mayan stone bearing an inscription, or some silver Teotihuacán jewelry; the newspaper clips recounting the story of the robbery and the museum catalogue pages where the piece was originally are even framed. You have more than a museum piece, you have a pirated piece. That is very elegant. Shortly, they'll appear in *Town and Country*. So that slug Garduño is the one who organizes the operations in Mexico, the big ones, not trash. One of these days Cuauhtémoc will win and we'll mount an archaeological police force and we'll screw him. You'll see . . . Do you have something against him? Want me to stop by?"

"No, I don't have anything, for now. Has there been some important robbery in the last few weeks?"

"Nothing that I know of, because those idiotic functionaries conceal them so as not to fry in public opinion. But there was something . . . The last one was the Museum of Anthropology job three years ago."

"Is there anything to rob around Acapulco?"

"The beaches, man. Those bastards are capable of going to the beach every day with a little pail and stashing away the sand," Murguía said.

Héctor went out to the balcony. An archaeological robbery? Estrella was on his terrace sunbathing. What was this guy up to? Héctor went to look for his binoculars. Estrella took off his dark glasses with a carefree gesture. This time, yes, Héctor had no doubt, the Cuban was looking at him. The detective backed into the inside of his room. The air conditioning was like ice, he said to himself. He went over to the controls and realized that that morning he hadn't turned it on.

He lay down with his eye wide open to contemplate the ceiling of the room. In the end, it wasn't bad under the bed, nor was it a bad idea, now that he'd come to his five senses, to put a couple of pillows down there.

"Do you want to meet Jerome up close?" Dick had asked him and Héctor hadn't responded. The North American reporter took this for a yes.

If it had seemed a crazy whim then, now it was clear that it had been a case of absolute lunacy. For the second time, he was exposed. The first time when he put the .45 in the Cuban's face to defend Dick and now, sitting by the pool of the Villa Vera drinking a Coke with lime while Dick contemplated the gringo in silence, a double gin on the rocks sitting between them.

"It's a true pleasure to see you," Jerome said, breaking the silence.

Dick nodded and with a gesture sent the waiter off for a new gin even though the first one hadn't been started. Jerome could not focus his gaze, his eyes seemed to escape him and not fix on the focal point; either he was very tired or he was up to his ass in cocaine. He was wearing a white three-piece suit and was fiddling with his sunglasses. Sunglasses were starting to annoy Héctor, they seemed to be the required tropical uniform of the enemy.

"You have an operation under way in Mexico," Dick asserted and, as if it weren't very important, started sipping his gin and looking at a couple of women playing tennis listlessly a few yards away.

"If that were right, I'm not the most appropriate person to say so. I've retired, I'm in private business," Jerome said.

"Private business doesn't exist. Company business exists. And Company business, if my memory serves, is all dirty. You Reaganites think everything that doesn't move or doesn't speak, in whatever corner of the world you find yourself, is booty. Sometimes you don't respect even that rule and you devote yourselves to slave hunting. You practice the art of patriotism mixed with the art of international commerce."

"There's nothing worse than a reporter who thinks he's intelligent."

"Come on, Jerome, tell me what you've got going in Mexico, and that way when the Democrats start crucifying your leaders, you can always jump out of the Roman Centurion uniform and say that you didn't like the story and that's why you leaked it to the press. How do you think I got here? Because another friend of yours tipped me off."

"I don't know how you showed up in Acapulco. But this is not Los Angeles. I'd be doing you a favor in advising you not to get involved in Mexican affairs. People are very touchy here."

"You have an operation in play in Mexico. Jerome, tell me something beyond what I already know."

"And what is it you know?"

"We reporters don't leak information. I remind you of the rules: CIA agents leak information, reporters gather it and make scandals. Isn't that right?"

"If you know something worthwhile, I suggest you sit down at the typewriter. I'll be happy to read it. You probably won't believe me, Dick, but I have been one of your closest readers," Jerome said, standing up.

Héctor buried his head in his Coke. Maybe no one would realize he'd been there.

"And what do you do now, Jerome? I'd love to quote you exactly."

The CIA agent turned his back on them, not bothering to respond, and moved away.

"Let's go see the cop who sings boleros, the businessman who robs archaeological gems, and the sailor who farms coconut oil," Dick said and drank down what remained of his gin in one gulp, then panted and finished off the other full glass. Héctor regretted not liking gin and drank his Coke shyly. This guy was absolutely crazy. So crazy, even Héctor's own craziness paled. If he followed him in the dance, he'd lose even his style.

Héctor Belascoarán got in the ocean and started swimming toward the void. He had left the reporter in front of the hotel taxi stand. He wasn't going to show his face again. He had plenty of logical reasons, he thought as he swam toward the center of the bay, but more than anything he had visceral reasons. The Genghis Khan method could have been useful at some point. You arrive, you tell them they're a bunch of pricks, simply idiots, that you already know everything, and you wait for them to react. But it wasn't very practical if you were trying to conserve your health. He suspended the rhythm of his strokes and started floating on his back. A wave, the product of a speedboat pulling a few bikini-clad waterskiers a hundred feet away, destabilized him for an instant, then calm returned and he closed his eye to escape the burning sun. Going out in the light was a stupid move, it put them on the alert, made them horny, agitated them, invited them to give you two shots in the face and rip your lung out with a kitchen knife; they liked you as a missing witness, a nameless cadaver, a stupid dead man without a wake. Héctor started swimming again. There hadn't been sharks in Acapulco for years. If he continued on his course, with a little perseverance he could get to Hong Kong, adopt a new name, wait for the last fragment of the British empire to crumble and open a taco stand in socialist China. It wasn't as absurd as it seemed at first glance.

He kept swimming.

Let's see, let that bunch of world-trafficking pricks try to follow him. Just by the trace of his piss in the ocean. He accelerated the rate of his strokes.

The entire problem was having a plan, a destiny. Giving meaning to anything. Grit your teeth. You don't have to open your mouth to think while swimming. He rested awhile, floating on his back. The beach was becoming tiny. There were no waterskiers or sailboats to bother him. There wasn't even a Coast Guard vessel asking him for his documents to let him leave Mexico. It wasn't such a stupid way of disappearing from any story. He started swimming again, now almost furiously, toward the Pacific Ocean.

One of his selves said to him: "Are you committing suicide?" The other answered: "So what if I am?" He kept swimming. He would never have to sleep under beds again.

Two hours later, a few robust Acapulcans from the municipal lifeguard service deposited him on the beach. Miraculously, they had saved him from drowning. One of his thighs was still stiff from the cramps and he had swallowed enough water to make his next two hundred Cokes taste salty. He was in a pretty good mood: if the Pacific Ocean, which was a bitch, hadn't been able to kill him, that bunch of idiots never could. He tried to stand up with the aid of one of the life-guards.

"Where the hell were you trying to go, kid? Out there is pure ocean."

"To Hong Kong, pal," the detective answered.

"See, jerk, I told you Hong Kong was that way," the lifeguard said to his colleague, pointing to the sun setting over the ocean, staining the blue with an intense orange.

Héctor got into the elevator trying to shake the water out of his ear and remembering the three versions of his will that he had written in his head.

He opened the door to his room and stopped dead. Two guys were wrestling with Dick near the terrace, trying to throw him over. One of them was smashing an ashtray against the hand grabbing hold of the hand-rail; he couldn't get it to let go. Héctor backed up a step, leaving the door open. They hadn't seen him.

"Come on, asshole. Let go," yelled one of the guys, wearing a sweatshirt with wide blue stripes, the kind made popular by the gondoliers of Venice. Dick drew himself up and threw a punch that hit him right in the lower abdomen.

The other character, a little chubby blond guy, pulled a knife.

"You're not going to cut him, idiot, it has to be just a beating," the guy in the Venetian shirt told him.

Héctor took a second step back. The struggle was drawing Dick close to the void. The tubby one put the knife away and kicked the reporter in the thigh. The latter doubled over, sliding across the floor. Héctor backed up a little more, staying out of the thugs' view. He leaned his back against the wall. He counted to ten. Then he made up his mind and entered the room walking normally. He made it to the bedside table. They didn't discover him until he had taken out the .38 and had it cocked.

"Look out, there's the other one," the tubby guy yelled.

The ersatz Venetian was distracted for an instant and Dick buried his head in his stomach. The guy buckled, Dick took the ashtray from his hand and hit him with it in the jaw; the guy started bleeding and slid to the floor. The tubby one had been hypnotized by Héctor's gun.

"You have no idea the cheap thrill I'm going to get from killing you, pal," the detective said to him.

Dick was laid out on the terrace, recovering. Next to him, the man in the striped shirt was trying to stop the blood and ward off fainting by taking deep breaths.

"You were late, what were you doing?" Dick asked the detective.

"I was going to Hong Kong, my friend," Héctor said, trying not to let the gringo notice that his hand was trembling. Turning to the thugs: "Who sent you? I'm counting to three, then I'm shooting, I don't give a shit if your blood stains the bedspread."

"The boss, Julio Reyes, it was a job, just an assignment, it's not our thing. He wasn't even going to pay us, it was something we owed him."

"If we throw them, where will they end up?" Héctor asked Dick. Dick leaned over the terrace.

"If they jump hard, with any luck they'll hit the pool;

if they screw up the calculation, they'll turn into shit against the asphalt."

"Is there a risk they'll fall on top of someone?"

"No, there's nobody down there."

"Well, now you know, it depends on your skill," the detective said to Tubby, digging the barrel of the .38 into his stomach.

"This one doesn't know how to swim," the "second-rate" Venetian said, who had moved close to his companion in hopes of rescue, and was holding up his pants.

"That, you should have thought of before," Belascoarán answered, pushing the fat one again.

"The best thing to do is for you to measure for him," Dick said to the guy in Spanish.

Héctor helped the bleeding man in the striped T-shirt to a seat on the handrail.

"Don't forget to take a running start," Dick said, calculating by eye where they were going to fall and moving his head as if they didn't have much hope.

"On your mark . . ."

"I suspect they'll break a few bones."

"It's only six stories," Héctor said as they went over the edge, aiming for the pool. He started trembling. He flung the revolver on the bed and tried to stop his hand from shaking by holding it with the other. A couple of giant tears came out and started to slide down his cheeks. Dick was trying to ascertain if they had broken the bones in his right hand with the blows of the ashtray and didn't notice what was happening. When he looked at the detective, he realized that Héctor was on the verge of collapsing.

"Lie down on the bed. I'm going to look for a bottle of gin. I think they broke one of my ribs."

"I don't like gin," Héctor said in the midst of his tears.

"Your loss," Dick answered.

The magical assailants must have made it to the pool, because no one in the hotel mentioned them and because when Héctor and the reporter went downstairs they didn't see anyone washing bloodstains off the cement. The small orchestra was rehearsing, tuning their instruments. Héctor wondered what bossa nova they would start with. "Corcovado" would be very good. They ordered two grilled lobsters to celebrate survival.

"Doesn't yours taste a little strange?" the reporter asked.

"Mine was the first one you ate," Héctor answered.

An hour later, they were in the emergency room in the government hospital in Acapulco; Dick was on the brink of death by poisoning. Héctor hadn't been able to eat his lobster, his stomach was closed, and he had limited himself to drinking a couple quarts of pineapple juice.

As he roamed outside the intensive care unit, watching a group of doctors moving around the reporter's body, filling it with probes every time he opened the door, Héctor, who no longer believed in accidents, decided that from that moment on he was going on a hunger strike. He had no intention of being poisoned.

VIII

"Justice loses?"
"Yes, every once in a while."

Justin Playfair to Mildred Watson
(*They Might Be Giants*)

Nostalgia goes through three phases. In the first one the memories are so close, so near, so three-dimensional that they can be evaded with a good dodging, a good feint that leaves them behind, writhing in the past. Then come the days in which the memory hurts like a bad headache and the scenes are relived and reheard like drums in the middle of the brain. Finally, the nostalgia becomes stupid, sad, painfully pleasant. Persistent, instead. The broken raindrops sliding down the glass, the wind rustling tree branches, a solitary swing swaying in the park, all the clichés of loneliness summon it. But that nostalgia, even with its tenderness, is no less obstinate, no less malevolently carcinogenic.

Héctor knew plenty about nostalgia, it had filled his head on the flight home. It all came at a gallop when the plane started to hover over Mexico City. The great spectacle of the unending sketch of colorful lights moved him and a couple of tears came out of his good eye. The erratic, geometric drawings, the great carpet of light, the green lines outlining the city, and the things

growing with the descent, the towers, the parks, finally
the jungle of rooftops.

The only problem was that nostalgia operated in a
vacuum. You could not return to what did not exist.
The city that had been his had escaped into the void
at some point over the last months. You can't return
to what doesn't exist, but you can long for what you
had.

Apparently, he had returned to Mexico City to find
himself in safe territory again, and he was discovering
something he had always known. If any unsafe territory
existed, this was it. The fears that accompanied him
were born here.

Dick had remained in Acapulco, recovering, stuck
in a Puerto Marqués hotel under a false name, posing
as a rock singer in post-alcoholic reclusion and, in
contradiction, accompanied by half a dozen liter bottles
of gin, and the solemn promise that he wouldn't drink
them all on the first day. Estrella had stayed behind,
too, and the truth is Héctor didn't give a shit. Estrella
himself would make sure that justice came to him and
he'd wake up someday lying in a rotten alley with two
shots in his back and an astonished expression on his
face because, after all, even he was not immortal. Goodbye, Estrella.

It was drizzling. He took a cab. Mexico City seemed
more hazy than usual through the windows. Héctor
was returning to the same city that at times seemed to
him like another one. The same city . . . When the car
stopped in front of his house in the Roma neighborhood, the drizzle had turned into a downpour. Five
feet out the door and he was drenched. As he shook

off the water like a dog, he found a note stuck on the door to his apartment: *I have to see you urgently. Carlos.*

He went into the house to get a raincoat. On the refrigerator door, a new note: *The ducks are fine. I feed them every day, they're pigs. They're under your bed. Alicia.*

He opened the bedroom door without making a noise. The ducks detected him quickly and approached, quacking. Héctor smiled at them. If they were sleeping under the bed, he might have to sleep on top and for one damn time, for functional reasons, he would throw off all that stupid paranoia.

He went back into the rain.

Carlos was in the kitchen having a *café con leche* and dunking a couple of croissants in his cup. He laid out a photograph for Héctor.

"Where did this photo come from?" the detective asked.

"Do you recognize him? They told me you would recognize him."

"Yes, I've been watching him for a week. He's younger, but he's the third from the right, next to the gringo carrying the M one and the soldier with the field radio ... How old was he in this photo?"

"Count. It's from nineteen sixty-seven."

"Then twenty-eight ... And the place? I've seen this place before, in other photos."

"It's a little village in Bolivia. Do you recognize the adobe school with the zinc roof? That photo must have gone around the world two thousand times in one week. It's the Higuera school, the place they killed Che."

"And what was Estrella doing there? What's that uniform? According to you, what's this guy in the photo's name? Did he have something to do with Che's death?"

"Yes, he had something to do with Che's death. The photo is taken in La Higuera on October ninth of sixty-seven. His uniform is from the North American Rangers, who were training the Bolivian army. But he was not a Ranger, he was a CIA agent who'd been in Bolivia since August of sixty-seven with a North American passport. See what he's got hanging from his shoulder?"

"Yes, it's a camera . . . Is that a wide-angle lens?"

"No, it's a macro; if you look closely, you can tell the camera is a Nikon. He photographed Che's diary with that camera. He was taking pictures of the diary in the house of a telegraph operator named Hidalgo when the petty officer Terán entered the school and shot the two bursts that killed Che . . . Earlier, this man had interrogated Che alone. Che was wounded, lying on the ground, your friend slapped him, Che tried to get up, but he was wounded in the leg, the Cuban ran out of the room, he was afraid of him."

"Where did you get the photo?"

"A friend gave it to me," Carlos said. "A pal who knows this guy who before calling himself Lisardo in Bolivia was named Lázaro . . ." Carlos consulted a few notes he had on a little piece of paper, ". . . Barrios, and who was a bouncer in a cabaret in Havana and an informer for Batista's police. And later he was Gary Betancourt, North American citizen and CIA agent. They told me that he's called Luke Estrella now and that you would know a little about that."

"Who told you?"

"A friend of a friend of the Cubes. The guy who gave me the photo and the message."

"What's the message?"

"That after Che was killed, the guy you're following entered the house and cut the hands off the cadaver."

"That's the message?"

"That's the message, that after Che was machine-gunned, the guy you are following entered the house and cut the hands off the cadaver."

Héctor was thinking, looking at Luke Estrella, who seemed content in the photo.

"The Cubes?"

"The Cubans."

"Are they following him?"

"You should know," Carlos said. "I'm the messenger. That's just how mysterious the affair is. A pal in whom I have a lot of trust comes along and says give a message to your brother. I listen to the message and I ask him where it's from and he says: from the Cubes. You sure? I say, and he says definitely. I leave you a note and I give you a message. Now I'm starting to feel like lending you a hand and beating the hell out of one Gary Lisardo."

Héctor picked up the photo and turned it over. Luke Estrella–Gary Betancourt–Lisardo–Vasco–Lázaro Barrios smiled at the camera, his white teeth blazed in the sun, his sunglasses raised over his forehead. Slightly defiant, arrogant, a lottery winner, trafficker of blanks in wartime occupation . . . Behind the group, you could make out the green spots of the mountains, over the tiles and the miserable stone walls of the houses. Che's corpse must have been somewhere around there.

"Did they say anything else? Did they say they wanted to see me?"

"Just the message."

Héctor walked over to his brother's refrigerator to get a drink, but his head was in another place, in other years . . .

The ducks had worked the miracle: he was sleeping on top of the bed. That was the first thing he noticed. Then the phone rang.

"He's arriving in Mexico City on the Mexicana flight out of Acapulco at twelve tonight," Alicia said.

"Thanks," Héctor answered.

"The ducks . . ."

"Would you like to speak to them?"

"No, I was just wondering if you found them well."

"Yes, perfect."

There was a brief silence, then she hung up.

Héctor stayed in bed, just waking up. Estrella would haunt him, follow him to the end of the world. He could never liberate himself from the guy who took the bloody hands of Che Guevara for a ride in his suitcase. The time had come to visit the psychiatrist.

"Why don't you whack him and the affair dies just like that?"

"Because if I whack him, I'm never going to find out why he came to Mexico. Besides, I suppose one can't go around just killing people out there."

"And besides, you're afraid to execute a Christian cold, right?" Gómez Letras asked.

"It has occurred to me that they might kill me first," Héctor replied.

"No chance, it's enough that they shoot you full of holes every time."

"That's what I'm saying."

"Why don't you let me help straighten out this disaster you've got in your head. Maybe I'll even understand it."

They were in the Chinese café, the usual secondary base of operations. It was growing dark. Héctor hadn't gone up to the office, he had sat down there to meditate and he'd met with Gilberto. The best officemate in the world, a guy who managed to make the weird seem normal. Gilberto would see to it that he never forgot that the country was real, that the stories that crossed through his life were real, that everything was so real that the only unreal thing was oneself. That reality was real even if it didn't seem so.

"You've got a CIA guy running around Acapulco like a swine and the son of a bitch even steals a piece of pyramid to give to the gringos ... That's what those slugs do. They steal the pyramids little by little because they want to put them in San Antonio, that's what my sister-in-law told me, and once they have them there, they'll say the Aztecs first passed through the United States, and it was just a few second-rate Aztecs who went on to Mexico; a few paltry, sluggish Aztecs, the

poor cousins of the ones who stayed up there, who
are the top Aztecs . . . And then, you have that guy and
you don't know what to do with him . . ." Gilberto said.

Héctor nodded.

"That guy wants to screw the nation," Gilberto said.

Héctor nodded his head.

"But there's more, right? Then let's kidnap him and
give him a hard time, like making him eat pure tamales,
not giving him one beer, not anything, and we won't
let him take a shit and in five days that guy will tell us
everything up to the name of the stupid mother of the
grandma of the hero of the country of those guys, the
Duke of Wellington, the one who screwed the French
at Waterloo."

Héctor sat there staring at him.

"What I think is that you don't know what it is you
want to do," Gilberto suggested. Héctor tried to smile
but couldn't.

"That's part of it," Héctor replied.

"That's what I thought. In any case, better to see it
without knowing what to do than to suck cock the way
you have been over the last few months."

"At that, I leave the check for you," Héctor said as
he stood up.

"The detectives before were good, these days they're
worth pure dick," Gilberto said as his goodbye.

Héctor didn't take offense. On the street, he hailed
a cab and left for the airport. Estrella seemed like a
cunning bride who never let herself be trapped. As
the taxi went through the viaduct, the detective tried
fruitlessly to make his hands stop sweating.

*   *   *

This time, Estrella did not go from the airport to a hotel, but instead took a taxi that dropped him in front of an elegant house in Las Aguilas; a maid opened the door. From inside another taxi, Héctor believed that a few yards back, behind the maid, he could make out a familiar face. Who the hell did that face belong to? Fortunately, the taxi driver was a man of few words and did not engage him in chitchat; they waited together as a torrential rain fell over the car.

"That guy's leaving now, boss," the helpful taxi driver said, waking the detective with an elbow.

True, Luke Estrella was approaching a radio taxi accompanied by the owner of the house, who was covering him with an umbrella. Héctor tried to concentrate on the character following the Cuban. Chubby, with a mustache with upturned points. He'd come across him some other time, laterally, in as miserable a story as this one. His name was Ramón Vega and he was the publisher of the only significant chain of pornographic magazines in the country. Of course, he, too, was of Cuban origin.

"Shall we follow him?" the taxi driver asked, now fully playing his role.

"To his hotel, and then to sleep," Héctor answered with a yawn.

*   *   *

Luke Estrella's name was not Estrella, but Gary Betancourt, and in his time, he'd been Lázaro when he was a cabaret bouncer and Lisardo, temporarily, when he wore a Ranger uniform, without that impeding his having been Valdés-Vasco, known as Vevé in Dick's complicated story.

But Estrella who wasn't Estrella was launching a grand CIA operation in Acapulco, and also fixed the prices of cocaine, was the judge of a beauty pageant, had cut the hands off Che's body, ate breakfast with a thief of archaeological pieces, and, by night, visited the czar of pornography, who was indeed a fellow countryman. He had an assistant chief of Acapulco's Judicial Police and a retired sailor for accomplices, he wore white linen suits, five of which he kept in the closet, and he had murdered Alicia's sister.

At this point in the résumé, Héctor wasn't really sure whether he wanted to break both his legs with a baseball bat or offer him the job of planning management for Imevisión or Televisa, the Mexican television monopolies. No doubt he would run them well. He would probably also be very capable in managing the public relations for some PRI candidate for the Senate or he'd make a good manager of a chain of grocery stores. Estrella, the versatile; Estrella, the systematic; Estrella, the inscrutable, behind those stupid dark glasses.

Curiosity had its limits. If you abused it, it became depleted. If the doubts outnumbered the questions, you didn't want to answer them anymore but rather forget the crossword puzzle, toss it for being too complicated, and busy yourself taking flowers to your neighbor on the seventh floor who was newly divorced, had a son still in the crib, and sobbed her heart out every night.

On the other hand, Héctor's options as a pursuer were more than depleted. Unless Estrella had been trained in the Disney World spy school he had to have recognized him, and if even so he persisted in his maneuvers, it had to be because he didn't give a shit if Héctor followed him. Estrella had to be sick already of seeing a one-eyed guy in a raincoat stepping on his shadow, and if he wasn't, still worse, it meant that the stupid maneuver that the CIA was assembling in Mexico was so big (as if they were going to rob the statue of Tláloc, all eleven tons of it) that it had been previously agreed between the president of the republic and the International Monetary Fund serving as the guarantor of the operation.

That's what Héctor was thinking in an orderly way, in contrast to his usual chaotic jumble, as he waited for Estrella to board a Mexicana plane that would take him to Morelia. Alicia had advised him in the early hours of the morning and Héctor, more faithful to his routine than a public bureaucrat threatened with personnel cutbacks, showed up for the appointment. He hadn't been able to sleep much in a night of lightning anyway. He had gotten it into his head that it was the night of the deluge and he wanted to see the flood that would do away with Mexico City once and for all.

It hadn't been that bad: just a few collapsed houses, two hundred injured in a neighborhood where a drainage canal had overflowed, and two people were found dead after having been trapped inside an automobile on the Beltway.

Estrella didn't even seem damp. Héctor decided to let him run around the country alone. Half an hour later he called Morelia and passed the Cuban's information to a retired theater actor, a friend of his, and asked him to check it out in the name of the love of art. Surprisingly, his actor friend called him the next morning, said Estrella was returning to Mexico City and told him that his jaunt through Michoacán had been brief. From Morelia, he had traveled by car to the ocean, on barely passable highways. He'd stopped in a little fishing village near the Guerrero border and then had begun his return. The actor hadn't followed Estrella, he'd limited himself to asking the chauffeur of the tourist taxi who drove him.

"And did he spend much time looking at the ocean, Marcelo?" Héctor asked.

"A good while," his friend said over the phone. "He and the state chief of police, who accompanied him."

"Shit," the detective said to the phone after his buddy hung up.

IX

Loud and deserted streets are rivers of darkness that will lead to the sea.

Maples Arce

It was still raining the next day and Héctor lost Estrella again. The Cuban entered the Hotel Berlin through the front door, upon returning from his jaunt to Michoacán, and never checked in, probably just headed out the back and walked through the parking lot. And if he wasn't boarding a plane, not even Alicia could find him. Héctor declared himself defeated and went to his office to sit in a rickety armchair and watch the rain.

It was raining with particular fury, the wind whipping raindrops and gushes against the window, wanting to demolish the glass. The street was empty, the cars had surrendered to the attack of the downpour. Somehow, as he lit his umpteenth cigarette, Héctor felt at ease. The rain sent one inside oneself, created a thick curtain of *outside*, invited patience and the fireplace, solitude and reading, pleasant memories.

It wasn't so bad, after all, breaking free of Luke Estrella. How many times had he said that in the last week? He rummaged through the strongbox for a multivolume novel by a German author that he had saved for a day like this. The book was called *The Wizard* and promised to tell the story of a strange character set in the final year of Nazi Germany. Next to the book were two old packs of cigarettes and four or five sodas, providentially placed there in anticipation of a day like this one. If he had a slight cold, the fantasy would be complete. Detectives with colds on rainy days. Worthy books, cigarettes, and soft drinks. A blanket would be nice.

Héctor Belascoarán Shayne sank down into the pink Mexican armchair that Carlos Vargas was finishing, opened to the first page of the book, and immersed himself fully in the stories of others. One's own stories weren't good for much.

He read for about an hour. Outside, the rain had grown more intense. And if Estrella got lost for good, all the better. What an absolute and total wonder if the Cuban would vanish from his life. He read for another half hour.

The detective carefully contemplated the window. Then he placed the books, cigarettes, and soft drinks back in the strongbox and went out, carefully fastening his raincoat, convinced that getting wet would be useless, that he had no idea where to find Estrella, that it was absurd to go and get drenched this way. But he was also convinced that if he gave up, Héctor Belascoarán Shayne would break into a thousand pieces and no one would be able to put them back together.

The storm received him in the doorway, spattering his face with rain.

*   *   *

Dick appeared at the door of the house at dawn, emaciated but smiling broadly. Héctor sneezed to welcome him; he had a cold.

"I will never eat lobster in my life again, man," he said in Spanish.

Héctor got back into bed. The ducks roamed freely around the reporter's legs; he pulled a sweet roll out of his pocket and threw it in crumbs over the rug.

"You lost him, right?" Dick asked.

Héctor nodded. "But my guardian angel found him for me. A while ago my brother called and told me that some friends of his told him to tell me that he'd be eating lunch today in the Café de Paris."

"How curious that we have guardian angels," Dick said. "I called in to the magazine and they told me that Betancourt was at the Hotel Princesa, that my casual acquaintance in the State Department had left me a message."

"Aren't you surprised by how many people have an interest in our following Estrella-Betancourt?"

"I couldn't care less if they're manipulating me. I do that to other people every day. I want Betancourt. I want him tied and wrapped in a raspberry-colored bow . . . I need a couple of beers to finish pissing out the poison."

"What was it? What did the doctors say?"

"They never figured it out. Who cares? But even if I don't know who poisoned me, I want Betancourt more than before."

Héctor agreed. So did the ducks.

*   *   *

The city was in electoral effervescence. Slowly it had been filling up with posters and graffiti proclaiming a list of candidates apart from, and clearly antagonizing, the PRIs. Every once in a while Héctor wanted to find the proof, in one of the painted graffiti, that his brother, Carlos, had been involved in the affair. Several had the style, if not Carlos's, then certainly of his generation of painters:

Men born to be henpecked vote PRI.

Would you lend your old bicycle to the PRI candidate for this district? Then why are you going to vote for him? Long live Cuauhtémoc!

With a little confidence, this time we'll break free from that ball of rats. Cardenista Committee, District 11.

The neighbors on this block will not tolerate fraud. Enough!

From the taxi, Héctor contemplated the walls that spoke. Dick startled him.

"Does Cardenismo stand a chance?"

"You're asking the wrong guy. Before devoting myself to Estrella, I was living on another planet. I don't know, it seems like a real novelty. Usually, no one gives a damn about the elections. Everyone in my office is going to vote for Cuauhtémoc. Carlos, Gilberto, Villareal, otherwise known as El Gallo, the engineer. Me too, I think."

They had spent the morning in a technical conference with Merlín Gutiérrez—El Mago— Belascoarán's

electrician and landlord. Gutiérrez had rented a suitcase of electrical devices for them and saturated them ·
with instructions that Héctor believed he half understood.

The taxi left them two blocks from the Hotel Princesa
on the side street off Reforma. They waited patiently
for Estrella to walk out the door on his way to lunch,
which occurred around 2:30. They entered looking like
a hybrid between conspirators and bricklayers in
search of work. For five thousand pesos, they found
out which was the Cuban's room. "Señor Esta, of
course, Room 207." For thirty-five thousand, they got
a double room next door; for ten thousand more, the
manager suffered a dizzying attack of amnesia. Then
came the plumbing labor.

The bathroom mirror gave way to the other bathroom mirror in the adjoining room; they dismantled
it with more patience than skill, and installed the micro-
phone on the line of the air conditioner of their neighbor's room.

"You think we're going to hear something?"

"I'm sure we'll hear him sing when he gets in the
shower."

Héctor started to sneeze loudly. Dick went to look
for his suitcase and took out a bottle of gin, as if he
thought the alcohol would ward off viruses.

"We're very visible at this point, don't you think we
should disguise ourselves?" he asked the detective.

"Short of dressing as a Chinese peasant girl, I don't
know what I would do about this eye," Héctor said,
pointing to the patch.

*   *   *

In the afternoon, Estrella-Betancourt lay down to take a siesta. Around 5:30 the phone rang. Héctor, who was in the bathroom urinating, ran to the earphones that they had connected to the tape recorder.

"Whatever you want, my colleague," the Cuban said into the phone. "No problem . . . Same time, same place . . . but, of course, my brother . . ."

Then he hung up and whistled parts of "New York, New York." The faucet in the Cuban's bathroom sink started flowing. Strange sounds. Was he brushing his teeth? A couple of soft knocks on the door, Estrella didn't turn off the faucet, but he did leave the bathroom, closing the door. Muddled sounds, a woman's voice saying something indecipherable in the distance. Dick entered the bathroom and with his eyebrows asked Belascoarán if something was happening next door. Héctor affirmed it and offered to share one of the earphones with the reporter. Finally a clear sound, the bathroom door opening:

". . . to do a lot of things, my queen," the faucet was turned off, "but I never stopped thinking about you. Even in my dreams."

"You're such a liar, Ramón," a woman's voice . . .

Ramón? And when had he met this one?

"I tell lies to the customs officers, my life, but how could I lie to you if you are a princess?"

"He's an old-fashioned bastard," Dick whispered. Héctor nodded.

"Come on, Ramón, order something from the bar."

"I've got a little bar right here, doll, what do you want?"

"A piña colada with spiced rum."

"She's a moron," Héctor said. Dick nodded.

"Aren't you hot? Take off some of your clothes while I get some ice."

"What nice pajamas, Ramón. Are they silk?"

"Yes, why the hell not, they have to be silk," Héctor said.

"Let's see, my love, let me unbutton your blouse."

"*Ay!* I'll unbutton it, but don't look at me like that, turn around."

"She's gone shy on him," Dick commented.

"You've gone a little shy on me," Estrella said.

"That's it, don't look at me and I'll start handing you my things and you look at them and start imagining everything, okay?"

"She better be careful or Estrella will steal even her shoes," Héctor said.

"Don't you have a brassiere, my life?"

"I don't need one, big man."

"Look at the familiar way she's treating him now; when they started they were using the formal *usted*," Dick remarked, interested in the variations of the language.

"Your panties are pretty," Estrella said.

"I wore them for you. Now you take off your pajamas without turning around, Ramón."

"And the shoes, my queen?"

"Those I keep on, because if I don't my legs will look fat, and I want to do it standing it up."

"Standing up, my life? I like it in bed."

"That guy has balls," Héctor remarked.

"But are you really going to please me?" she said.

"Hey, what the hell is this!" Estrella said, his tone suddenly changing.

"Don't you like it?" she said.

"Fucking hell! I can't believe it, you're a guy."

"*Ay,* but not as much of a guy as you."

"Get off me, stop screwing around."

"*Ay,* what's wrong, Ramón."

"You're a man, shit!"

"Now they've screwed Estrella," Héctor said.

"Now Estrella is screwed," Dick said in Spanish, shaking his head in a gesture of sadness.

"You didn't know?" said the woman who now turned out to be a man.

"See, Dick, what happens if you're not careful," Héctor said to the reporter, extracting the moral.

"Oh Christ!" Estrella said.

"Now that we're here like this, all naked, I won't tell anybody, couldn't we take advantage of it?" he/she said.

"Fine, why not," Estrella said. "But I get to stick it in you."

"Fine, why not," he/she said.

"See how everything works out in the end," Dick said.

"Who would have thought it?" Héctor asked, taking off the earphones.

The meeting at who knows what time turned out to be at nine at night in the warehouse district. Héctor kept a prudent distance, but saw Estrella inspecting two big cargo trucks accompanied by a guy with a little mustache and a double-breasted suit. It was cold; Héctor left the twosome talking in the warehouses and went home to feed the ducks.

The birds were content and hadn't missed him too much; they had learned how to climb up on the kitchen table on a path Alicia had made for them out of cardboard boxes, upside-down slippers balanced between benches, plates, and clothes hangers. Before long, they'd know how to use the neighbor's microwave to make a sandwich and El Mago's iron to warm the bedsheets on winter nights. OP had diarrhea, JJ liked the pâté (which proved Héctor's theory that Mexican pâté was made of the liver of anything else—that, or the ducks were cannibals). Héctor watched them maneuvering around the kitchen table, changed the turbid water where they drank, swam, and pissed, and left to put some César Portillo de la Luz boleros on the record player.

There were a couple of letters thrown on the floor near the record player. Perhaps El Mago, his landlord, or Alicia had left them there. One had a Puerto Vallarta postmark. It was from the woman with the ponytail. Laconic: *I'm on the way. How are the ducks behaving? You would have liked the ocean. Me.*

Héctor had his doubts in that respect. Moreover, he thought, never again would he try to get to Hong Kong by swimming, there were more auspicious ways to travel.

The other one was anonymous and typed on an old typewriter, the ribbon fading from use and the dryness of the climate. It wasn't as sparing as the missive from his woman.

The man you are following is involved in trafficking arms destined for the Nicaraguan contras. You can be sure of this fact, it is reliable. Since he cannot smuggle them in directly, he is using Mexican drug traffickers in a cross-operation. The price that someone has set in order to launch the operation from Mexico is that part of the arms be used here for another equally disturbing affair. Needless to say, you should be extremely cautious. Please destroy this note. It is sent by a few friends who share your same interests in this matter.

Héctor read the note twice and applied the flame of the lighter to it; he took advantage of the moment to light a Delicado. He let the paper consume itself in the ashtray. He smoked peacefully as a smile began to form on his face.

The guardian angels were working overtime.

Dick informed him that Estrella had spent the day in the hotel, answering phone calls in which no one made himself clear. He/she who liked to make love standing up had disappeared by dawn. Dick gave the detective a grocery list that included three six-packs of Tecate, two liter bottles of gin, and a lot of newspapers; if he could get the provincial papers, all the better. As he recited the list, the reporter sneezed violently. He seemed to have caught a cold.

"Let me go over the tape two or three times, maybe there's something that makes sense in the idiot's conversations. I have the impression we're getting close to the date."

"You be the detective, I'll be the shopping lady," Héctor said.

The difficult moment was crossing the hall. Between the door to his room and the elevators was Estrella's room; it was possible that the Cuban would bump into him. So Héctor could not avoid putting his hand over his gun as he passed the door and got to the stairwell, went down a floor, then took the elevator from the fifth floor to complete the descent to the peaceful street.

This time everything worked out fine, but as he crossed Reforma, without waiting for the light as usual, dodging the cars, he got the impression that a couple of suits were on his back repeating his experiences. He jumped up on the median, avoiding a city bus, and looked over his shoulder. They were about ten feet away and the two were watching him, not the cars. He pulled out the .45, cocked it, and showed it to them. It was an act of calculated insanity. Anyone who saw him would think he was playing with his nephew's early Christmas gift; no one draws a gun in the middle of Reforma these days, unless it's a federal cop. Nonetheless, placed under the barrel of the .45, the two suits got the message and retreated the way they had come, jumping. Adding more glory to Héctor's maneuver, one of them ran into a baker's delivery boy's bicycle and fell to the ground, ripping his pants. The detective no longer cared to know more and accelerated his pace.

His fears were metaphysical, essentially metaphysical. If he didn't walk on the grass, he would live to be eighty-five. If the neon light didn't touch him, he would have a son. If for one second he could avoid being hit by that Datsun's fender, he would be immortal again, he said to himself, and leaped forward. The wake of the car, passing at forty miles an hour, didn't even ruffle his hair. It was clear that he was immortal.

At least until next time.

X

Let's imagine it for a single instant: The social classes in Kandinsky's head. The denial of the denial in Dick Tracy's head.

Roque Dalton

There's nothing like not knowing who is the victim and who is the executioner. Fear is not just about the worst foreboding of what is going to happen to you if you're not careful, it also has to do with not knowing where you are or what your friends will say about you when they find you dead. Fear, therefore, is a kind of reflection, a kind of meditation. Useful, but not too practical.

Who was pursuing whom? Was Betancourt-Estrella playing with them? What damn purpose could all this have? Were the guys who had tried to follow him outside the hotel waiting for him somewhere? Did they have them identified, located, fitted with names, houses, addresses? Were they pretending they were following them but weren't, rather that they wanted them to think that they were following them but that the detective and the reporter had managed to throw them off? Could they throw them off? Or did they really have them constantly under a microscope lens?

Héctor walked the last three blocks to the corner of his building, looking over his shoulders every two minutes. A nervous pain started throbbing in his left kidney. It was not nephritis, it was simple, vulgar terror. The light in his apartment was on. Shit. As far as he was concerned, they could stay; let them, whoever they were, be in charge of feeding the ducks. Just when he was on the verge of going off to sleep in the Northern Bus Station, and with a little luck, catch one to Ciudad Juárez, Alicia leaned out the window. Friday watched over the deserted island, Crusoe said to himself. He went up the stairs more calmly, though conserving a small doubt in a corner of his head that made him draw the .45 and knock on the door of the apartment with it.

"I was feeding your ducks," Alicia said, smiling, ignoring the gun.

"Yes, I already know that. By the way, you never had a sister."

"And how did you come to that conclusion?" Alicia asked, looking at him affectionately. She seemed to have come straight out of the 1960s, ten minutes after a Joan Baez concert. A certain air of tie-dye, though not exaggerated. Her loose hair shimmered around her head as she moved about the room; she wore an embroidered white blouse and a very full white skirt.

"Nowhere. Around, adding things up." Héctor went to the kitchen, looked in the refrigerator and discovered he had fewer than half a dozen Cokes left. He would have to go shopping. "You, who hired me and who feeds the ducks, could have at least stocked the refrigerator with Cokes."

"On an expense account?"

"Something like that," Héctor said, sitting on the rug.
"Do you work for the Nicaraguans or the Cubans?"

"Do you really care? Would it change anything?"

"Sometimes I think I get into these jams out of curiosity. That when you forget how a story started, there's always the curiosity of how it will end. Fine, then that's why, out of curiosity."

"For the Nics . . . And I had a sister. What I told you about Estrella is true, he killed her."

"Did she work for the Nicaraguans, too?"

Alicia didn't answer.

"Do you think you could get me one of those photos of Sandino, smiling, with that enormous hat, the ones they use on the anniversary posters . . . ? I always wanted one," Héctor said and walked over to the record player. Neither "Stardust," nor boleros. Nothing less than Beethoven's Ninth.

Alicia moved to the bedroom, taking off her blouse.

"Hasn't it occurred to you that I might have a venereal disease? You could ask, couldn't you?" Héctor yelled after her.

Alicia turned in the hall and smiled at him. Héctor confirmed that her breasts were still lopsided. He turned up the volume as the Philadelphia Orchestra attacked the first chords and for a few hours, he said goodbye to fear.

"And this one, who's this?" the woman with the ponytail asked, pointing at Alicia, who was sleeping naked and without covers beside the detective.

Héctor opened his healthy eye, noted the advancing storm, and said, "Her name is Alicia, this month she's my boss, I work for her." He rubbed the sleep from his eye, the fog was beginning to disappear.

The woman with the ponytail opened the window. The light blinded him totally.

"Don't you get cold sleeping like that?" the woman with the ponytail asked Alicia.

She had entered suddenly carrying a couple of suitcases which she left beside the bed. One of her black boots kicked Héctor's bare foot sticking out from between the sheets.

Alicia was waking up and was trying to cover a little of her nakedness as she did so. A breast escaped from the sheet.

"Where does that leave us? Who is this lady?" asked the woman with the ponytail.

"It's my mom," Héctor said.

"Your fucking mother," the woman with the ponytail elaborated. Radiant, the freshness of the dawn on her face, no trace of road dust from the trip on her, smiling maliciously.

"Excuse me if I interrupted something," Alicia said, looking on the night table for a pack of cigarettes that wasn't there. "Excuse me, but last night when I arrived, there was no one else on this side of the bed."

"Okay, my dear, the headliners have arrived, it's time for the understudies to exit the stage," said the woman with the ponytail and she started to undress.

Héctor started looking for the same cigarettes that weren't there, not daring to look at either of the two women.

"I do not like waking up like this," Alicia said, jumping out of the bed. She walked to the bathroom, gathering her clothes. Then she turned her head. "Good luck," she said to Héctor.

"Belascoarán, if you tell me that you missed me, I'll poke out your good eye with one kick," the woman with the ponytail told Héctor.

"I missed you," Héctor answered. The woman with the ponytail, beaming, was finishing undoing the last button of her pistachio green blouse and smiled, showing him simultaneously a lilac brassiere and two gleaming rows of teeth.

"Come on, move over," she said, taking off her skirt.

Héctor finally found the cigarettes on the floor by his side of the bed, but lamentably they were tangled up in Alicia's underwear. Humbly, he moved over and renounced smoking. For the moment.

"Three things, I have three things . . ." Dick said.

"When I left yesterday, two guys started following me . . ." Héctor began, but obviously Dick's things were more important.

"Three things. One: It's going to be the day after tomorrow, Friday. Two: The exchange is made in two trucks that arrive, two that receive. There's a third truck that will go straight to Acapulco. Three: Estrella is an intermediary in the operation, but he has to put up the money."

"What's in the trucks? Where are they going to arrive? If he's an intermediary, why does he have to pay?"

Héctor asked. "And besides, two guys followed me yesterday."

"That's why you're an entire day late, I already finished what was in the minibar while I was waiting for you, and I can't let them restock it because I can't let the maid in so she won't see the mikes . . . Asshole," Dick said.

"I didn't see them. I was circling around outside the hotel today and I didn't see them. But if they had something to do with Estrella and they recognized me, why didn't they warn him so he could take off?"

"Estrella left the hotel last night, partner," Dick said.

"To where?"

"I have no idea. Nor did I dare ask him. They came to get him and he left, without discussions, without talking about anything, without comment. They knocked on the door and said 'Let's go, Ramón,' and they left. He didn't come back all night. I think he took his bag, he travels light."

"And why didn't you dismantle everything and leave?"

Dick was thinking. "I suppose he left at the same time I was emptying the minibar . . . Did you bring the beer?"

"Yes, but I'm afraid they're not cold."

"And now what's next?" Dick asked.

"I suppose that while you drink them, I'll think it over. And I'm going to think it over somewhere else, I don't like this hotel. Find me in the office or at home," Héctor said, saying goodbye.

But he didn't go to either place, he started walking along Reforma toward Chapultepec Castle. A couple of hours later, leaning against the stone balustrade of the old colonial pile, peering at a city that was trying to hide itself in the smog, he joined together a series of ideas:

Estrella disappeared with extraordinary ease, but they also found him very easily.

The operation would take place in the garage in the warehouse district. It was an ideal location for the trucks that would be swapped.

The sentimental life of the detective Belascoarán Shayne was as confused as always. He was absolutely in love with a woman who was no longer quite so much in love with him and who insisted on wearing her hair in a ponytail, as if she wanted to recover the grace of adolescence. And she did.

Estrella trafficked in arms for the contras, that was what was going to be exchanged in the warehouses. Arms for something. Drugs obviously, and Estrella was going to pay the drug people and distribute the arms. Where was the third truck going? What did the Acapulcan friends have to do with all this?

Who were the guardian angels? He had a vague idea, but he preferred not to go too far into that. They were out there, they existed, period.

The breasts of Alicia and of the woman with the ponytail blended together in his memory. That could be dangerously serious. At this point, Dick would be completely drunk. That could be serious, too, though not as much.

A retired detective was an intelligent detective. Detectives belonged to novels; when they escaped from them, they were caricatures that roamed the city phantasmagorically, not knowing what to do on windy afternoons like this one.

In two weeks, he had not managed to hate Estrella. He was a caricature of evil, of whom much was said, but the eternal distance between the narration and the character always remained. There were two Estrellas: one, the one from the movie that began with the assassination of Che and who would later become a character dedicated to nefarious machinations, one of which was killing his wife; and the other Estrella, the caricature whom they'd been following these two weeks and who had screwed a transvestite because it was better than jerking off. He wasn't scared enough of him to hate him.

That led him to the problem of fear. Fear came and went. He was so damned dazed that his fear had become a collection of scattered sparks in the midst of a general sense of dullness.

Héctor Belascoarán Shayne, detective, was a stranger. A stranger in motion. Stranger to everything, stranger to everyone, stranger to himself. He couldn't quite recognize himself, he couldn't quite love himself. And since he neither loved himself, nor stopped loving himself, he couldn't be too careful. He was absolutely sure that in this story they were going to kill him.

An enormous crowd of protesters was marching toward the city center on Reforma Avenue. He watched it unfold little by little. Students? Land-grabbing colonists? Cardenistas? The murmur reached as far as the top of the castle. The city was not to blame for his being a stranger.

Estrella was a pig; a drug trafficker; a whitened mu-

latto, or rather a fake black, not truly black and therefore respectable; a torturer for pleasure; a murderer
of women; a son of a bitch who wanted to ruin the
Nicaraguans. If he could remember all this the next
time he saw him, he would settle someone else's bill,
Héctor told himself. This protest could be against the
PRI, it could be a Cardenista protest, it could be a
protest against Estrella and his shit-eating friends who
wanted to screw the Nics. Héctor lit a cigarette, shelter-
ing the flame of the lighter, and left the castle to be in
solidarity with the protesters.

Dick was clipping newspapers with a little pair of
scissors with a black handle that had come out of a
magic case. Very precisely, he stuck the clips in a note-
book with orange covers. In the last few days in hotels,
Héctor had seen him repeat the process again and
again and he couldn't resist his curiosity.
   "What the hell are you cutting out?"
   "Things that I read in the papers. I'm collecting them.
No one will believe I was down here if I don't."
   "What things?"
   "Mexican stories. Look . . ." he said, handing him the
photo album of clips.
   Héctor started turning the pages. *Teeth Lost While
Leaving Wedding* was the title under the one that re-
counted the story of a citizen who, after getting married
in Pátzcuaro to a woman by the last name of Jiménez,
got a blow with a brick in the kisser from an unidenti-
fied hand on the very steps to the door of the church.

The Wall Fell on Top of Him While Doing What Was Necessary was the headline of the story of another native of the city of Oaxaca, last name Abardía, on whom a wall fell one stormy day while he was very peacefully taking a dump against the traitorous thing. *In Search of a Good-Looking Girl Who Has Not Been a Whore* read a classified in Monterrey's *El Porvenir* and offered the phone number of a pharmacy and the last name Martínez to take references. *There Has Been No Honeymoon as Próspero Won't Let Go of the Pitcher* was the headline of the story in a Chilpancingo daily, recounting how Próspero remained drunk eleven days after his marriage and no one could stop him from drinking. *Priest Raped 40 Children and 1 Acolyte* headlined the item in *Alarma*, and did not explain how the acolyte had also been had by the clergyman. *Wounded in the Buttocks While Cutting Prickly Pears* said the headline of a story which transpired in Zacatecas that explained that Carlos Aguirre had been shot in an intimate area by some hunters, although it didn't explain why he was going around with his rear in the open air just to cut prickly pears.

Ceremoniously, Héctor returned the notebook.

"If we get out of this alive, no one's going to believe they're real anyway."

Héctor looked out at the street through the window of his office. It was raining again.

"Don't you have the urge to write?"

"Every urge in the world. I'm bored with this Mexican vacation. It'd be better if you'd give me a story soon," Dick said, opening a beer and watching the foam spill over the top.

"Tomorrow night, in a warehouse. We should look for a spot to see everything clearly. If possible, a place where we can hear what they say."

"I'm ready on my side, I can take a beer and drink it on the way. That's why I love Mexican laws, they've got nothing against one drinking beer on the street."

"That's the one thing we're missing," Héctor said.

The woman with the ponytail was brushing her hair in front of the mirror and Héctor Belascoarán, sui generis Mexican detective, couldn't stop watching the brush go up and down, constructing forms, making simulated waves that then disappeared, creating the tail that she would later proudly swing like the last car on the train. She sensed that something out of the ordinary was coming and she looked at Héctor in the mirror.

"Are you saying goodbye to me?"

"It's a just-in-case goodbye."

"What are you mixed up in this time? Even the ducks know something strange is going on."

"Then why don't you ask the ducks?"

"I asked them, they answered me and I didn't understand shit . . . I asked you if you were saying goodbye; if that's so, don't say anything and let me leave first. That's my role. I disappear. I am and I'm not . . . We could get married before disappearing."

"Do you have any interest in inheriting my bookcase, my X-ray and blood analysis collection, my notebook of my dear old mother's recipes?"

"Your Charlie Parker records."

"I hereby give them to you. See? Now you don't have to marry me. Anyway, the last time we decided to get married, neither one of us made it to the judge. The witnesses had to throw the party alone."

"Are things going to get ugly?"

"I don't know, the truth is I don't know. Can I give you a task? If something accidentally happens to me, can you get on the motorcycle and run over a guy named Estrella? My brother, Carlos, might be able to tell you where to find him."

"Is he the mulatto in the photos you've got around? The ones hanging in the kitchen?"

"That's the one."

She came out of the bathroom looking at the sunlight streaming through the window; on the way she picked up a cup of cold coffee she'd left there before.

"If we got married, I couldn't be a conventional housewife. For example, you'd have to keep cooking while I recited López Velarde's poems to you, and now for two. You'd have to cook for two. And what's more, I throw my clothes on the floor when I undress. I always forget to buy gas, pay the light bill . . ."

Héctor stared at her. Shit, how he loved her. She was the ideal woman for a suicide pact. The risk was that if he proposed it, she was sure to say yes. They would have to be sane to get married. They would have to be absolutely crazy to live together.

They walked hand in hand along Insurgentes. They were starting to put up the Christmas windows. The rain began, first a few sparks of water, then a regular downpour; they got drenched. The detective's cold came back. Héctor was getting nervous, this afternoon

stroll seemed out of a movie with a happy ending. Fear
sank into his body. This time, he was afraid of being
afraid. They dined on hamburgers and french fries in
a plastic dive on Ínsurgentes. They went into Sears and
meticulously reviewed the record section, not looking
for anything specific. Suddenly, Belascoarán slipped
away while she was buying a camera.

As he walked he tried to erase his tracks, to lose the
woman who was following him. Who was following
him? He went into a theater. If the box-office woman
had asked him his name, he would have given her a
false one. He half watched the movie, as all one-eyed
people do. He couldn't really figure out what it was
about.

The gentle tap the stewardess gave him on the arm
woke him up. He smiled stupidly, trying to explain to
the girl in the Mexicana uniform that she was part of
a dream, but she'd gone off down the aisle. They'd
begun their descent.

How the hell had he gotten on a plane? A plane
bound for where? Why couldn't he be here? Where
was he supposed to be at that moment? If the ticket
were to New York or Havana or Mérida, then he would
be far enough away from the date on Friday afternoon
with Dick to go spy on the swap of Estrella's trucks.
He looked for the ticket in his coat pocket. It was in
the name of Francisco Pérez Arce, and it was a one-
way ticket to Tijuana.

He tried to look out the window but a woman with

a child was in the way. At any rate, his stomach told him they were descending. What day was today? The boy's mom who was blocking the window had a paper on her lap. *La Prensa*. Friday. The whole day was Friday. And the time? He looked at his watch. 10:35. In the morning, of course, it was day. He hit himself on the forehead. Fine, hell, Tijuana was as good a place as any to set up a frog hatchery, a poultry farm, a grocery store chain, a publications distribution house, a chain of Ping-Pong parlors, a refuge for the demented, a home, a family. Three sons. Without doubt, he would name them Mickey, Donald, and Bugs. A late homage to the amount of shit he'd read on his way through college.

Almost unintentionally he turned his gaze back to the paper she'd let fall on her knees. Without wanting to, he'd seen something else as he stared at the date. He separated his gaze from the paper, looked in his coat pockets; surely he had a novel. No. His hand, without willing it to, picked up the paper and turned the pages. The woman stared at him balefully. There it was, damn it. There was a photo of Dick on page seventeen, a passport photo, but smiling. Beside it was another of the corpse. *Gringo Reporter Murdered by 17 Bullet Wounds, 3 Fatal*, said the seventy-two-point headline.

Dick would have liked to have clipped the item. He probably would have liked to begin his report with an item like that one. If the detective hadn't escaped, he might be writing it right now. But he hadn't escaped. He hadn't said, "I'm going to escape, I'll be back in a while." If he had, he didn't remember it. Are you less of a son of a bitch if you've got a bad memory? He had said to Dick, however, "See you in a while, I'll be right back," and he hadn't gone back. Héctor Belascoarán felt his hands starting to tremble. He was not going to keep a date. He was not going to keep a date with a dead man.

The pilot's voice announced that they were landing at the Guadalajara airport. Passengers going to Tijuana should remain on the plane a mere twenty minutes.

He'd be damned if he wouldn't get there, he'd get there running, crawling he'd get there; on a bike in the middle of a storm he'd get there; on horseback or on a mule, he would get there. Nothing could impede him. Nothing could stop him. Scared to death, trembling, but he was going to show up at that date with his dead friend.

XI

Where will you go that the night won't grab you?

Rolo Díez

If he had looked carefully when he went home to pick up the artillery, he would have noticed that the ducks were sending him a serious warning sign. But Héctor was not in his finest hour. He was in a hurry to keep a date, and when one is in a hurry, one puts one's tie on backward, forgets the theater tickets, doesn't whistle the right tune, puts salt instead of sugar in one's coffee, falls in love with the wrong woman, spatters one's pants when urinating, or one encounters an armed man, in the middle of the room, aiming with a bear-hunting rifle.

"I'm only going to shoot you if you start getting nervous," said Reyes, the bolero-singing Acapulcan cop. "Moreover, I don't care about your story, nor do I want to hear it. And if possible, I'm not going to shoot you because I happen to like your records. I have a lot of them, too, the same ones. You have good records ... The truth is I'm just doing a favor for a pal. In reality, they're just paying me to take a truck to Acapulco without letting anyone see it or open it or touch it. But they're asking me to do a

favor and I'm doing it ... So I'm doing you a favor.
I'm not going to kill you, I'm only going to ask that
you turn around and one, two ..."

He'd been tied up with wire to a chair. He tested
the resistance before opening his eye. When he did,
Estrella was there, before him, waiting.

"It's a job," Estrella said, as if apologizing, as he
studied Belascoarán's sad face. "The difference is that
I am a professional and you are not. But the bottom
line, my colleague, is that this is business, no hard
feelings."

But even though it was only that, business, first he
spit on the detective, then slapped him. Héctor's head
swayed. His wrists hurt more than his head. Estrella
moved to hit him again, with his open palm, as if in
slow motion. Héctor tried to hide his head, but there
was nowhere to send it on vacation. The blow fell on
the same cheek. Now it did hurt. The second ones are
the ones that hurt, Héctor thought, and a tear welled
up. Fear or impotence? It was very important to know,
the shitty question was not rhetorical; but the Cuban
didn't give him time to reflect.

"Since when, kid, does a professional make so much
noise when he's being followed? You think I'm stupid?
Putting a one-eyed man to tail me? That's straight out
of the circus. And I was thinking you were the visible
and that behind you was the invisible. But the only
invisible behind you is your ass."

Héctor nodded just as the third blow landed. He felt the Cuban's ring make a small slash on his cheek.

"You know, kid, I like slapping. It's like a pleasure, like eating fruit, my colleague. That's how good it is."

Héctor nodded again. The Cuban made a move to slap him again and Héctor closed his healthy eye. The blow never came. Estrella had stopped himself, and opened his arms. He repeated the gesture and the detective kept watching.

"Ooonly youuu . . ." the Cuban sang with open arms, the hand of the slap that never came extended in the air.

Héctor seized the opportunity to look around. They were in a huge empty cargo warehouse. A couple of floodlights lit up what seemed to be an isolated area where there was a half-open office with a couple of chairs, a desk, and a large jug of purified water inside. He was tied up in one of the chairs; in the other, the Cuban had placed one of his patent leather boots. The boot shone strangely under the light.

"Come, Chato," said Estrella.

To his name and from the shadows, a character who took great pride in his nickname emerged, a tiny piece of a nose embedded in two enormous cheeks and sunken eyes.

"Take him and kill him out there, far away . . . like the gringo. Come back soon, before midnight."

Héctor felt himself urinating. Fortunately, he hadn't had too many refreshments that day and he didn't make much of a puddle. Estrella turned away without looking at him and was lost in the darkness.

"Fucking *gusano*," the detective cried. "Come back

here, you prick. If you're going to kill me, you owe
me an explanation of all this idiocy."

"Oh, face it, it's all terribly complicated. If you only
knew. The thought of explaining it to you exhausts me,
One-Eye."

"I'll trade you. I'll tell you who hired me to follow
you. Come back, asshole! *Gusano* faggot, tell me!"

Estrella reappeared from the shadows.

"The truth is, my brother, I don't give a shit. It could
be anyone. The current owner of El Tropicana, Barbas,
who God in his glory confuses. My boss, who wants to
protect his money. My mother, that brute, who follows
my steps from heaven, and pays stupid Mexican detectives instead of hiring professionals from Detroit."

"You're going to swap drugs for arms, right?"

"Look, I'll tell it to you quickly and if you understand,
fine, and if you don't who the fuck cares how informed
dead people are? I buy cocaine from some, from others
I buy arms with the cocaine."

"And if you've got money, why don't you buy the
arms from the second group of guys and save time?"
Héctor asked, putting on his best bewildered face.

"See what an idiot you are . . . Because they buy arms
in the United States, and I can't go around buying things
up there. But that's what contacts, connections, soul-
mates are for. So I buy drugs in Mexico and with that
I buy arms from the States, and I make a lot of people
happy. We're all friends, buddy. Later I send the arms
to some friends, who pay me to do that, to have those
arms reach those friends; but not all of them, colleague,
just part. And I give the other part of the arms to other

friends for letting me play on their diamond, for lending me the bat; the balls are mine, kid. Get it? None
of it? Shit. See? I told you. You'll die just as ignorant
as when you were alive."

"And what crap are the Mexicans who you gave the
arms going to pull? No, wait. They'll take them down
to Michoacán—" And Héctor shut up, thinking about
how he would die smarter than he had lived. Estrella
left without granting much importance to the expression of an illuminated angel on the detective's face.

El Chato didn't waste time untying him; with unimag-
inable strength he lifted the chair, detective and all,
and loaded it into the back of a small van. Then he got
into the driver's seat and started the engine.

Leaving the shed, a series of fine drops of rain began
to fall on the van. El Chato cursed under his breath.
The windshield wipers didn't work. Héctor was trying
to keep his balance in the chair. They were on the
outskirts of the warehouse district. When they got to
the second stoplight, El Chato seemed to have decided
their route. Héctor was thinking that dying in one place
rather than another made absolutely no difference to
him, when a motorcycle stopped next to the driver's
window, and a gloved hand smashed El Chato's head
with a wrench. The big man collapsed over the steering
wheel, and Héctor had a laughing attack.

"What are you laughing about, asshole?" she said,
taking off her helmet and swinging her ponytail in the
rain.

Héctor couldn't respond. He didn't know how.

* * *

"And who do you work for, young Chato?" Héctor asked the character tied up with wire to the chair in the back of the van.

"He's mute," said the woman with the ponytail.

"Well, for a mute, he was carrying too many papers. Just look," Héctor said, showing El Chato what he had pulled out of his bag a couple of minutes before. "Michoacán state police, holy shit. Let me guess ... You are the one who's going to accompany the arms to be unloaded in Michoacán. You are the one who's going to seize them. You are the one who's going to tell the press that the Cardenistas were dealing in contraband arms with who knows what dark motives. No. You're not going to say that, someone more photogenic will say it. You are just going to take the arms to the coast and there you'll play at inventing an unloading. The papers will do the rest. There's just one thing you don't know that I do know."

"What do you know?" she asked, driving very professionally. No showing off.

"That this Chato knows too much and they're going to kill him when they unload, or shortly thereafter. That there can be no witnesses to this story. That for the provocation to work, there can be no poor boys out there to later tell the story to someone one day when they're getting drunk in a Puerto Vallarta hotel."

"What a drag, to be poor and mute," she said.

"Maybe you fucked him up with that wrench."

"I gave it to him gently," she said, smiling proudly.

"You better drop me off on the corner," El Chato said. "You can't stop it. They already tipped off the reporters. Even if there aren't any arms, there'll be a scandal for the Cardenistas. They'll be screwed all the same. A few arms will pop up anyway; these because they thought they were pretty, and the boat and everything, and they're not even Mexican arms. Just because the Cuban put the operation within our reach. Better to let me off here."

"No, sir, because you know what we're going to do? We're going to give the press a Chato tied up with wire to a chair. A Chato who will tell them the whole story. See what a mess this is."

"There's no way to give me a chance?" said El Chato, with an expression that said that any way he looked at it his future was not going to be very bright.

"Like what?"

"Like I give you everything in writing and you give me twenty-four hours to clear out. When all is said and done, I don't have shit against the Cardenistas. My boss was with Cárdenas during the previous campaign."

"I'll think about it seriously. It strikes me that you could become an honorable man again."

"If I were you I wouldn't believe it. When I hit him in the head with the wrench he made a face of a man with bad instincts."

"He made the face of a PRI idiot. And besides, he was going to kill me."

"How do you know, if you were tied up in the back?"

"Because lately I've been learning a lot."

* * *

A strategic operation is characterized by the incorpo-. ration of a dose of wisdom and a dose of insanity in equal parts. Héctor did not know how to launch one. For him, all war operations were beyond idiotic, all deceiving, all nightmarish. But now he was going to try, because in Mexico, just having faith and the good guys on one side of the fence is not enough. It's not enough to count on reason, self-esteem, utterly justified rage, the power of Hegelian dialectic, and that kind of thing.

In this stupid country, Pancho Villa formulas like a horse and a lot of balls clearly aren't enough; behind it you need the artillery of General Felipe Angeles; the morals of Guillermo Prieto, who was secretary of the treasury in the nineteenth century and died in poverty; the sense of direction of a city bus driver; the originality of the Aztec king Cuauhtémoc, who spouted historical quotations when they were burning his feet; the good star followed by the Avila brothers, eternal, triumphant trapeze artists of the Atayde circus; the skill of Herme-negildo Galeana not to dislocate his wrist when using a machete; the patience of the holy Niño Fidencio; and the marksmanship of someone from Tomochic. And therefore, the .45 and the .38 he had stored in the fridge were not enough; he needed a rifle he had in the closet, a heavy coat for the rain, a new patch for his bad eye, some drops for his good eye, a recently sharpened kitchen knife; and, of course, the one small van they'd stolen from El Chato was not enough, he

needed at least two or three more. Héctor resolved
the problem of the ideological arsenal and the practical, but with respect to the van, he was stumped. Fortunately, the woman with the ponytail had hidden
resources, probably the result of having had a million-
aire father at some point in her life.

"Let's go to the corner and we'll rent them with
drivers and everything. Do you have money? Because
you can't rent vans with a credit card."

"Not a dime," Belascoarán said, finishing tying the
knot of the threads of the war he was preparing.

There are complete mariachi bands, half-mariachi
bands, mariachis with black uniforms and silver-plated
buttons, with popular uniforms, no uniforms, with
bugles, without bugles, with bugles and piano damp-
ers, with middle basses and a fat man with a double
bass, with three violins, one for decoration, or simply
with two. To liven up parties, for accompaniment, for
nothing but show, with real or fake guns, with their
own cars or base infantry. They swarm around the
outskirts of the remodeled Garibaldi Plaza attacking
pedestrians, reminding us that in all past times they
flirted better, screwed better, sang better; offering the
musical glory for the best and most bitter goodbyes
to departed and tormented lovers, the most bastardly
serenade and raising the barks of dogs to make the
future father-in-law turn green with rage, the most me-
lodious of the offensive seducers with antiquated and
necessarily romantic techniques. (If it worked for Jorge

Negrete and Pedro Infante, the great ranchera singers, why not for you? Are you perhaps more cowardly than the aforementioned?) They move toward the cars like casualties of unemployment, thereby revealing themselves as equals and equally as afflicted as we are by the Monetary Fund; even if they're found dressed as mariachis and not as real Mexicans. And they offer themselves so that you might hold hands with the past, return to the old rituals, which really do work, and attack accompanied by a singing army. That is precisely what it was about. No euphemisms.

Nothing half-assed, a holy war sung with mariachis. An authentically Mexican war, born of the best national traditions. The way Dick would have liked it for the end of his report.

With three hundred thousand pesos up front (half down, chief, in case you say later the serenade didn't work and we have to walk back), Héctor hired four mariachi bands, a total of twenty-six musicians, with silver-plated suits, two sloshed fat men with trumpets, all with real guns but no bullets (there Belascoarán had to be very precise), to sing for half an hour wherever the gentleman told them to. Surprises work, right?

The entourage advanced in procession toward the eastern part of Mexico City. While the woman with the ponytail drove the stolen van, Héctor, looking at his watch every so often as if the time of the date would slip away on him by a dirty trick, was instructing the natural leaders of his four mariachi bands about the order of battle and the appropriate repertoire. First, they would set themselves up comfortably in an arc. Then he would open the garage door and there they would enter one by one. First piece: "The Song of the Black Woman," later your choice, mariachi by mariachi. And then, right at the end all together, "The Sandal." Singing the refrain two times, the one that goes "The sandal I throw, I will not pick up again."

The rain had stopped when they took the viaduct. There weren't too many cars, the crisis and the autistic suggestion of "Come, little dear, lock yourself up with your TV, it will give you the warmth that humans take from you" was doing away with even Friday nights, which were in turn finishing off Saturday nights, which had in turn eliminated (I don't give a shit if tomorrow is Monday) the still better than hopeless Sunday nights; when you really lived even if you didn't know it.

When they turned down Río Churubusco, the woman with the ponytail had convinced him to practice "Mule Drivers Are We" with the mariachis and, like a furious lunatic, detective Belascoarán Shayne was howling Cuco Sánchez's wonderful lyrics:

If after all, we cooome from nooothing,
And into nooothing by God we will retuuurn . . .

What would you say if when it is very quiet, inside a legally rented warehouse and being Cinderella's hour, twelve midnight, while two trucks with machine guns, grenades, and mortars are very harmoniously being unloaded and are being swapped for a few dozen well-packed packages of cocaine, with their plastic intact and the purity guaranteed by a competent chemist who received his degree at the University of Guadalajara; all very legal, then, with no suspicion, and the Acapulcans count the dollars and the gringos weigh the coke, then ten thousand mariachis enter playing "The Song of the Black Woman" and one foolish one-eyed lunatic starts shooting a rifle at random? What would you say if the one-eyed man is also yelling incomprehensible things, almost howling, as he shoots? And instead of stopping playing, the mariachis continue entering the ware-house, the ones in back pushing the ones in front, blowing the bugles and giving it to the violins, and the one-eyed man fires everywhere at the same time and then the Acapulcan druggies get nervous and think someone has pulled a double operation on them and start firing at the gringos with the arms; if they were nervous since before and their hands weren't ticklish on the triggers and they start firing, too, one group against the other instead of firing at the mariachis in front of them who now finally realize that practically nobody likes the music and start shooting their guns, because they'll be damned if they're going to run around with fake guns and blank cartridges with every son of a bitch loose in this city, and they were educated sentimentally by the best Luis Aguilar movies where first you shoot in the air, then you ask questions and later you shoot in earnest. And Estrella, meanwhile, flees to the back part of the warehouse. And one of the one-eyed man's bullets hits him in the back, near the spine, and Estrella thinks how can he die in Mexico, of all the places he's been . . .

And what would you think if in the middle of this mess, while the mariachis in the back insist on making their entrance playing because they, too, were being paid to play, and the detective finds himself wrapped up in a skirmish with the ones who were going to take the trucks with arms, the ones who carry Honduran passports even though they were born in Managua, a woman in a motorcycle helmet enters and hurls two bottles of gasoline onto the truck and a sudden blaze fires up? What would you think? Huh?

In the middle of the fire, the shots, the cries, Héctor thought it best to put a little distance between them, because within a few days a good number of cops, a ton of Miami mafiosi, a truckful of Nicaraguan contras, and twenty-six mariachi musicians dressed in black with silver-plated buttons would be looking for him.

Outside, on the street, in spite of the rain, the neighbors were applauding a truckful of firefighters, the walls of the warehouse were burning. The flames mingled with the flashes of photographers. Who had called the press? The guardian angels were working overtime. Héctor saw himself reflected in a car window. What was he doing there? The pain of the fear, near his spine, paralyzed him. The woman with the ponytail took him by the arm and squeezed. They went off. The detective was limping. They could still hear the shots.

The apartment was quiet, the omnipresent ducks would be sleeping. The woman with the ponytail went into the kitchen to make coffee. Héctor slipped into the bathroom on tiptoes and looked at himself in the mirror. He decided to shave. As he did so, dry, with a

disposable razor, he said to himself: "Fine, okay; it's
not bad winning every once in a while. Winning even
if it's halfway. Good. It feels fucking great to win every
once in a while," and things like that. It wasn't working
at all. Dick wasn't around having a gin.

There was one small debt left. One day he would
meet other Estrellas on the other side of the world,
around the corner. And that day, he'd kick them twice
in the balls and sing "Only You" to them.

As he shaved, he discovered that the cut on his cheek
was starting to bleed. It wasn't a big deal, a slash about
one or two inches long. How had it happened? Estrella's ring when he was slapping him? Wiping the
blood off the corner of his mouth, Héctor Belascoarán
tried to force a smile. The sun was coming up. The light
entered softly though the bathroom window. From the
kitchen, the woman with the ponytail offered him some
coffee; Héctor asked for something cold with lime. She
told him they were out. Héctor told her to look under
the sink, in the secret hiding place; in the emergency
stash where he kept another automatic .45, selected
novels of Hemingway, a first-aid manual, a can of Astu-
rian pork and beans, and two Coca-Colas. He heard
the woman's guffaws.

He opened the window. Sleepy children were going
to the corners to wait for the school bus. Maids on the
way with milk. Drunks going home. Industrial workers
starting the hazardous hour-and-a-half trip to the as-
sembly line. Adolescents absolutely lovelorn, convinced that they wouldn't be loved this time either.
Writers who hadn't slept well going out to take a walk
before getting into bed to dream with their eyes open

about the novel that wasn't coming out. Circus magicians mentally practicing the marvelous act that had kept them awake. Farmers without land coming from far away to loathe the bureaucrats of the Agrarian Reform as they stood in line. Remorseful suicides. Pregnant and early-rising mothers; teachers who pulled ingenious algebra lessons out of their hats; insurance salespeople who didn't believe in insurance; miraculous subway conductors; physicists who couldn't be like Leonardo da Vinci; journalists on the way home; lottery salespeople who would never win; FM radio station announcers on the way to the job, who knew that once again they would read false news and who dreamed of one of these days passing on the information that was denied them; proud old people who no longer knew how to sleep; nurses of the soul; stray dogs; unpublished poets; blacklisted film directors; democratic bureaucrats on the verge of being fired; rock drummers; compulsive Althuser readers; teenagers swaggering defiantly at six in the morning who couldn't stop believing they owned a city that adored them; Cardenista bricklayers, zealous conservators of the skill of laying bricks vertically without plumb lines. All the manufacturers of different metropolises, of apparently impossible futures, on their way to the routines pretending that they would be the ones to one day make the city blossom like a flower and become another.

He came out of the bathroom, took the refreshment in his hands, and went into the bedroom preparing to pack a bag. He would go to the woman with the ponytail's house for a few months. At least to throw off the mariachis. He would be so foolish as to marry her, as absurd as to be a Mexican detective, as strong as fear. And if he left everything? With the artillery and the two volumes of Victor Hugo's *Les Misérables*, he'd have more than enough. That and the ducks . . . He went to the window again, drawn by the light. It was starting to rain. Why weren't there ever any rainbows in Mexico City? He liked to see the rain fighting with the light. He lit a cigarette.

Héctor Belascoarán Shayne found himself returning. Among other things, to the same city as before. A city the same as and different from the one of always.